Balancing the

Vernon Coleman

This book is copyright.
Copyright Vernon Coleman 2015. The right of Vernon Coleman to be identified as the author of this book has been asserted in accordance with the Copyright, Designs and Patents Act 1988.

Dedication

To authors and to five star reviewers everywhere. And, as always, with all my love to Antoinette who understands.

Chapter One

When Harriet first came across Deborah she intended only to mess with her life a little, to give her the opportunity to taste the pain she had caused her husband and herself; to feel just a smidgeon of the anguish she had brought into their lives. She had thought it likely that Deborah had destroyed their lives on a mindless whim, without thinking about what she was doing.

But when Harriet had studied her prey for a while, she realised that Deborah was a malignant woman, a cancerous growth doing enormous damage to society; contentedly breaking the hearts and minds of strangers without feeling, without a whisper of restraint, a flicker of self-doubt or a moment's hesitation.

And Harriet then decided that the only sensible, honourable, decent thing to do was to bring about her demise, to delete her from society in the same way that someone using a computer might delete a literal or a misplaced adjective. Those with a Shakespearean view of life might call it taking measure for measure. Those with an Old Testament turn of phrase would refer to it as taking an eye for an eye. Others might, I suppose, call it payback, revenge, redress or recrimination. Harriet liked to think of it as 'balancing the books'.

Deborah was a specialist one star online reviewer, an absolute star in the modern world of criticism, and, like most of her breed, she hid behind a pseudonym; so that she could dispense misery with no recourse; pain without responsibility. She reviewed books, films, plays, hotels, restaurants and everything else reviewable. And the one star review was her trademark.

Within the world of literature, her speciality, as she thought of it, was to do her best to destroy a book completely. She was not content to say simply that she didn't like the sound of a book (she hardly ever began one and had never read one through to the end) but wrote reviews (and headlines) which were designed to ruin. She did this anonymously, of course, abandoning fame and kudos for privacy and protecting herself with one of those anodyne, unoriginal pseudonyms which seem to be favoured by the 'ubercritic', and which are inevitably shared by a thousand others.

Deborah claimed to be a former teacher though it was not clear what she'd taught or to whom she had taught it. Harriet never bothered to find out. It didn't seem important and certainly wasn't relevant. Maybe she'd been a puppy trainer. She had views on many books which she had read and on many more which she had either looked at for no more than a moment or two. She was a keen reviewer of books which she had never looked at.

It apparently never occurred to Deborah that if she didn't enjoy a book (or didn't think she might enjoy it) it might, just possibly might, be because she wasn't the sort of person for whom the book was written. It never occurred to her that it might be her 'fault' if a book didn't tickle her fancy. It never occurred to her that it might be cruel to give a book a devastatingly damaging review because she was in a bad mood or cross because the book's supplier had failed to satisfy her high standards. It never occurred to her that if she didn't enjoy a book she might be well advised to keep her doubts to herself. It never occurred to her that in damning a book she had never read she would be sticking a dagger into the author's heart.

She had views on anything and everything and was always eager to share her simple-minded opinions and prejudices with the world. The world is now full of arrogant and illiterate bullies such as Deborah, and everyone is at their mercy. The Deborahs of this world are overwhelmed with disappointment, frustration (of every known variety) and a burning sense of personal failure and they obtain their only satisfaction by spewing venom at anyone and everyone within range.

In the old, pre-Internet, days the Deborahs of yesteryear would have been sanctimonious street gossips, obtaining their raw material by peeking through net curtains and then standing on their doorsteps to share suspicions, resentments, accusations, prejudices and plain old-fashioned lies with anyone prepared to listen. But today, the malignant gossip has been super-enfranchised and the world is her doorstep. She can sit in her kitchen and spew venom around the world through the endless variety of social media sites. She can do it anonymously and apparently without responsibility.

With a few stabs at the keyboard any ignorant fool can destroy a book and eviscerate an author. She can mark down a restaurant she's never visited or skewer a film she's never seen. The evil old bat who used to share her gibberish with a handful of like-minded idiots can now reach a global audience.

Sane and sensible people used to steer clear of the street gossip because they knew she was dangerous and batty (the twitches and the saliva dribbling from her chin were good clues) but the modern Internet gossip hides in the dark and spreads her venom anonymously.

The ravings of the mad witch living at No 13 were temporary and relatively harmless; quickly forgotten even by the other witches. But the anonymous ravings of the modern, ignorant and intemperate reviewer are permanent, damaging and sometimes lethal; a review written by a toxic, half-witted psychopath is afforded just as much importance as a review written by a skilled and thoughtful critic. It occurred to Harriet that it is sometimes possible for democracy to go too far.

Deborah had reviewed four books written by Mallory, who had been Harriet's husband, and she had given each one a single star. She had put much the same comment on all four books and she had done all these within a single five-minute period on the same day. The woman was clearly too egocentric to empathise with the author.

The words she had written bad been burnt into Harriet's soul: 'Not my cup of tea.'

That was it.

'Not my cup of tea.'

The same words, written four times; decorated on each occasion with a single star.

In the old days, a bad review in a newspaper or magazine might hurt a book but it would not kill it. For one thing, only the readers of that particular publication would see the review. And, of course, reviews published on paper quickly end up wrapping chips, stuffed in the rubbish bin or helping to light a fire.

In contrast, a bad review on an Internet site lasts forever and affects sales for eternity. Some one star reviewers seem to delight in having the power to destroy the sales of a book.

Like many of her colleagues, Deborah did not confine herself to reviewing books. She reviewed hotels, restaurants, holiday resorts, stately homes and a wide variety of retail establishments. When Harriet did a little research she discovered that Deborah had written over 400 reviews – and she found that virtually every one of those reviews had been accompanied by a single star. There was one exception. Deborah had awarded five stars to a device designed to make it easier to slice hard-boiled eggs when preparing a salad. With this solitary exception, she had spread her spite far and wide, and had shared her ample supply of venom among authors, kitchenware manufacturers, film directors, chefs and clothing suppliers. She was full to the brim with attitude and never short of a trite mal mot; from afar she seemed convinced that the world was forever waiting for her latest views on something or other. Some of her reviews were blatantly racist and some were overtly sexist but most were merely abusive and spiteful. All were full of spelling mistakes and basic grammatical errors. It is, thought Harriet, so much easier to criticise than it is to create. In the days before the Internet was invented Deborah would have got her kicks using a key to scratch the paint on new motor cars.

Harriet had never killed anyone before so she had to think for a while before she worked out the best way to get rid of Deborah. She thought it was probably vital for the reviewer's redemption that she should know who was killing her – and why.

It seemed to Harriet that if you're simply killing someone in order to steal something from them, or to stop them doing whatever it is that they're doing that you want them to stop doing, then the killing can be clean and quick. There is no need at all for the killing to be drawn out.

But if the killing is for revenge, and is designed, at least in part, to provide the killer with some relief, some liberation, some sense of necessary retribution, then it really needs to be as slow and as painful as it can be made. And the victim must know why he or she is dying.

Harriet felt the victim has to suffer if he or she is to stand the remotest chance of redemption.

And it seemed to her only fair that someone who has caused considerable suffering should themselves be exposed to a little suffering. She didn't think that anyone could possibly claim that to be an unreasonable, unchristian attitude. After all, the words 'an eye for an eye, a tooth for a tooth' come straight from the Bible and not from an old KGB handbook. Furthermore, in such circumstances it seemed vital that the person who is being killed should know that they are being killed (as opposed to suddenly not being alive) and to know precisely why they were being killed.

It would be terribly unsatisfying, Harriet decided, for a wronged individual looking for revenge to push someone under a train and have them die instantly without ever knowing precisely why they'd died or who had killed them. Under those circumstances, there would simply be no time at all to tell the 'pushee' why they were being deleted and probably not even time to tell them who was doing the pushing. What sort of relief (for the executioner) or redemption (for the 'executionee') could there possibly be in such a death?

Harriet decided that Deborah had to die for what she had done to Mallory and to prevent her destroying other people's lives. In Harriet's mind it would have been as wrong of her to do nothing as it would have been for a policeman to do nothing about a serial killer.

But since Deborah's crime was one not yet recognised by a society which is proving slow to catch up with the strange mores of an Internet controlled world, Harriet had to take on all the responsibilities herself. She needed Deborah to die as slowly as possible so that she could be redeemed. And Deborah needed to know why she was dying; so that she had a chance to repent. Harriet decided that she would have failed Deborah if she allowed her to die a sudden death.

She felt that it would, in addition, be good for Deborah if the dying was excruciatingly painful or, at the very least, extremely uncomfortable. But she was prepared to accept that the pain did not have to be physical. Fear, frustration and a feeling of helplessness can all be painful.

Harriet's problem was that she was very small and not very strong. Even if she wanted to she couldn't rely on being able to kill her victim by hitting her over the head with a brick or sticking a skewer into her heart.

Moreover, she wanted Deborah's death to look like an accident, so that the police would not start hunting for a murderer. She knew she would have to find a subtle way to kill the reviewer.

Chapter Two

Those who write reviews on the Internet always assume that they can preserve their anonymity by hiding behind their (often silly and invariably uninspired) pseudonyms. Even those who use their real names assume that their addresses will remain hidden and that they can write whatever they like without worrying that they will, one night, open their front door to find an angry author standing on the doorstep with a printed copy of a review in one hand and a steak knife in the other.

Neither group are as safe as they think they are for it is surprisingly easy to trace people these days.

People give away vast amounts of information about themselves without realising just what they are doing or what the consequences could be; they have no idea how modern technology makes it easy for people to find them and to learn everything there is to know about them.

And they have no idea how much harm their stupid, callous, thoughtless reviews do to other people's lives.

Enthusiastic reviewers, constantly desperate to share their opinions and exert their power, have no idea how many people would happily do them harm.

It is harder than it has ever been for anyone to hide these days, and the same Internet which appears to offer bullies the chance to write what amounts to little more than graffiti (while pretending that it is literary criticism) also makes it relatively easy to identify the bullies and to trace their home addresses. Search engines will find most people in minutes and what would have taken a private detective a week can be done in a fraction of the time by anyone with modest research skills.

Most one star reviewers are, by definition, extraordinarily egotistical and they've usually written letters to newspapers as well as writing reviews. Many newspapers still print the addresses of their correspondents. And, of course, local councils readily publish names and addresses of all those citizens who are entitled to vote.

Deborah had, of course, written all her reviews under a rather clumsy pen name but being half-witted (at best) she had also completed a section on the website in which she had listed a good deal of information about her likes and her hopes for the future. A study of these, alongside the reviews she had written, quickly gave Harriet a number of clues both as to Deborah's identity and the area where she lived.

Harriet, who had done a good deal of research for Mallory when he was working on his books, quickly discovered that Deborah was genuinely female, that she lived in a flat in a London suburb (she worked in an office and commuted into London every day) and that she was overweight (she had for years been looking for a diet book that worked).

Time and time again Harriet found that anonymous reviewers had included extraneous information which made it terribly easy to identify them. For example, one reviewer whom she identified had chosen to be anonymous but had, in various reviews, reported that she worked on the checkout tills in Sainsbury's, attended services at a local Cathedral and loved to take long walks on the nearby beach. When you have so much information it isn't difficult to identify an individual.

The deadliest reviewers boast endlessly and enjoy feeling important. They are so arrogant that they don't realise how easy it is for strangers to identify them. Some reviewers even put their nom de plumes on their Facebook pages. They perhaps do not realise that once they are identified, their deniability will disappear forever.

Harriet knew that if she'd been prepared to plough through Deborah's reviews it would not have been difficult to identify the individual who had helped to destroy Mallory's books. But she used a short cut to find her true name and address.

On her personal wish list Deborah had reported that she was desperately hoping to buy a filter coffee machine at a good price. She named the manufacturer and listed the model she was keen to buy.

From that point on it was terribly easy.

Harriet opened an account on eBay and put up for sale a coffee machine of the type Deborah wanted. She made sure that her machine was much cheaper than any of the others which were available. It was, she said, brand new and still in the box and packaging. She explained that it had been given to her as a present but was not needed because she already owned a similar item.

Harriet didn't own the damned coffee machine, of course. But no one would ever know that. She knew that once Deborah had taken the bait, and had submitted her order, she would have her name and her address. And so it turned out.

Having discovered that Deborah lived in a small terraced house in one of London's outer and unfashionable suburbs she caught the train to London on a Friday and found a small hotel in Sussex Gardens, just a short walk from Paddington Station. This part of London used to be quite a smart area but it's rather depressing now. All the once fine houses have been turned into small hotels and cramped bed-sitting rooms which are now described by optimistic estate agents as studio apartments.

Early on Saturday morning, Harriet caught the Tube to Deborah's home. She took with her a laptop computer with which she was, reluctantly, becoming quite adept. She had an idea that it would come in handy if she could somehow find a way to sit herself down next to her target. She had even rehearsed a short conversation that might enable her to start some sort of friendship with Deborah.

It seemed to her likely that a woman who spent so much of her life writing mean reviews on the Internet might be rather lonely and unlikely to have many genuine friends.

Deborah had a flat on the first floor of a two storey Victorian terraced villa and although she shared a front door with the ground floor flat, there were two push bells fixed to the doorframe. Harriet still didn't know what the reviewer looked like and for a short while she toyed with the idea of sending Deborah a bunch of flowers, or a pizza, so that she would be able to see who came to the door when the delivery was made. But it wasn't necessary.

There was a run-down Baptist church on the other side of the road and Harriet simply stood in the porch for a while and watched the front door to Deborah's building. She knew that if anyone noticed her they would simply think she was waiting for someone to come along and open the church door. She tried to look like someone waiting for a Bible study meeting; or a downtrodden woman waiting to be interviewed for a cleaning job. She had her laptop with her but it was in an old canvas shopping bag.

She had been standing there for little more than half an hour when a fat woman came out of the house carrying a black, nylon laptop bag and a large, thick plastic shopping bag that looked much stronger than the usual sort of bag they sell for pennies in the supermarkets. The woman was the ugly side of plain and dressed in clothes that looked as if they had all been bought by mail order by someone who still thought she was a size 18 when in reality she needed something built more along the lines of a tent or marquee. The woman didn't have much colour sense, either. Her jumper was a bubblegum pink with a bright yellow pattern on it and her ankle length skirt was a mustard colour. She wore sandals and even from across the road Harriet could tell that she smelt of incense. Harriet had never trusted anyone who wore sandals and smelt of incense. As soon as Harriet saw the woman she knew that this was Deborah.

Harriet followed the woman into the shopping street, a quarter of a mile or so away, and it seemed as though it were going to take all day to get wherever they were going. She had never seen anyone walk so slowly. Deborah stopped once or twice at little shops but did most of her shopping at a mini Tesco store. Harriet stood outside for a moment or two and watched her. It wasn't difficult to see why she was so overweight. She bought only packaged meals (the sort that people eat by themselves in front of the television) and didn't buy anything that might have contained a vitamin or any other nutrient.

While she was shopping, Harriet slipped into an adjacent charity shop and purchased a diet book for 50 pence. Harriet was not overweight but, for the plan she had created, she needed a book of some sort.

When she'd finished her shopping, Deborah headed for an overpriced coffee shop and, judging by the confident way she headed through the door, she seemed to be a regular there.

Harriet suspected that this was Deborah's regular Saturday treat, and her suspicion was confirmed when the woman bought herself two large cakes and a cup of coffee that had cream piled an inch or two above the rim.

A painfully thin, surly girl at the counter sprinkled something brown over the top of the cream and Deborah seemed keen on this addition for when the girl thought she had finished Deborah told her to do some more sprinkling.

Harriet was now standing right behind Deborah, who was totally wrapped up in herself and quite uninterested in what was going on around her. When it was her turn at the counter, Harriet ordered a cup of tea with a slice of lemon. The thin girl told her they didn't do tea so Harriet said she'd have a pineapple juice, which she knew they did do because she could see the little bottles in the cool cabinet. The thin girl had five gold coloured rings in each ear and one very large silver one in her nose and Harriet couldn't help thinking that the one in her nose must have made life difficult for her when she had a cold. The girl also had tattoos on her neck, though Harriet couldn't tell what they were.

Deborah chose a table for two near the back of the café and Harriet was delighted to see that although the table on her left was occupied (by a young couple who were too busy with each other to see what else was going on) there was an empty table on her right.

Harriet put her drink down on the table and instantly regretted not having bought something to eat. The drink looked very lonely on the table and it occurred to her, rather too late, that Deborah might feel warmer towards someone who, like her, enjoyed a couple of cakes with her drink.

She had to squeeze past the shopping bags which Deborah had dropped onto the floor next to her feet and the reviewer made no effort to tidy them up, even though she could see that they were in Harriet's way.

Although she still hadn't eaten her cakes, Deborah took her laptop out of its bag and put it reverently down on the table top, having made sure first of all that the table top was free of crumbs and coffee dregs. She had stencilled her name and a security number onto the computer's lid and Harriet now knew for sure that this was her target and she felt adrenalin rush through her body. Deborah opened up the laptop and turned it on. It was quite a new laptop, Harriet noticed, and probably one of the more expensive ones.

Harriet waited a few moments and then did the same with her own laptop. In another place, and at another time, it might have looked odd: two women sitting in front of open laptops. But here they were lost in a crowd. Harriet looked around and could see that at least a third of the customers had open laptops in front of them. Those customers who didn't have laptops were occupied with their mobile telephones. Only the couple on Deborah's other side were interested in each other; they were holding hands and doing a lot of smiling and cooing. The sight of them reminded Harriet of Mallory and for a moment she felt as though she wanted to cry but then she saw Deborah reach for one of her cakes and take a huge bite and somehow she didn't need to cry any more. Harriet pressed the start button on her laptop. While it purred into action she took the diet book out of her bag and put it down on the table next to her computer.

And there they sat, side by side, with their computers open and ready for action.

It seemed clear that this was a regular Saturday morning date for Deborah and, Harriet suspected, for many of the others who were busy tippy tapping away on their computers. Two dozen strangers all together, all sharing a communal experience, but at the end of the day all still strangers. She wondered what they were all doing; so earnest, bent over their laptops. She picked up the diet book she'd bought, flicked through it and put it down again. Then she pressed some keys on her computer and took herself onto a bookselling website. She had set up an account under another name and now she keyed in the title of the book she had bought. When the details appeared on the screen she sat back, as though puzzled by what to do next. She glanced to her side and saw that Deborah was still concentrating on her computer screen. She appeared to be writing reviews and Harriet wondered if this was where she had written her series of vicious reviews of Mallory's books.

'Excuse me,' Harriet said, leaning across. 'I'm so sorry to bother you, but do you know how to put up a book review?'

Deborah looked at her. She had thin lips and narrow, hard eyes. She looked mean. She wasn't the sort of person who makes balloon animals at children's parties or sits in a park feeding bread to the sparrows.

'I bought this book,' Harriet said, holding up the diet book. 'And I'm very disappointed with it. I want to put up a review.'

Deborah looked at her and a strange look appeared on her face. It took Harriet a moment to realise that she was smiling.

'You've never written a review before?'

'No,' Harriet admitted. 'Is it difficult? Do you know how to do it?'

'I've written lots of reviews,' said Deborah. 'It's easy when you know how.' She leant across and showed Harriet what to do. 'Just write your review in that space.' Harriet thought Deborah might turn away, as any ordinary person would. But she didn't. She peered at Harriet's screen as she wrote a scathing review and then gave the book three stars.

'Oh no!' she cried, reaching across and grabbing Harriet's hand before she could complete the review. 'Why are you giving it three stars?'

'It wasn't a terribly good book,' Harriet said.

'You said in your review that it was useless,' she pointed out.

'It was,' Harriet said. 'It's actually a pretty awful book.'

Deborah picked the book up and glanced at it. 'I can see it is,' she said. She threw it back down on the table.

'I thought I'd give it three stars because it isn't very good,' Harriet said.

'One star,' said Deborah firmly. 'Give it one star.'

Harriet looked at her and raised an eyebrow.

'It hasn't got any reviews yet,' Deborah explained. She sounded envious. 'This is the best time to post a review.'

'Post it?'

'Put it up. That's what we say.' Deborah seemed incredibly pleased with herself, and was unbelievably patronising. 'When you're putting something on the Web, you're posting it.' She did the smile thing again. At least Harriet thought it was a smile. She wouldn't have lasted long playing Mother Christmas in a department store grotto. The children would have run home screaming. Harriet decided that she was definitely going to enjoy killing this woman.

'I think I could soon be inducted into the reviewers' hall of fame,' Deborah whispered.

It occurred to Harriet that Deborah thought of herself as something of a celebrity; a genuine diva. And she realised that diva-like attitudes have now filtered all the way from the top to the bottom of society. The glorious arrogance we associate with divas started at the opera, went to Hollywood and then filtered down through policemen, doctors, receptionists and Post Office employees. It occurred to Harriet that if the diva-like attitude has now reached as far down as Deborah then it has reached the mud at the bottom of the pond.

Harriet tried to look impressed. 'I suspect not,' she thought. 'Not unless they have a posthumous section.'

'There's a hall of fame for reviewers?' said Harriet, genuinely surprised.

'Oh yes,' she said, lowering her voice and speaking rather reverentially. 'Only the most famous reviewers are in the hall of fame.' These were, to her, clearly heroes, legends and role models. 'Some of the most successful reviewers have written thousands and thousands of reviews.'

'I bet you've done a lot of reviews,' Harriet said.

'Hundreds,' Deborah replied proudly. 'I've written hundreds of reviews.' She looked straight at Harriet and looked genuinely happy; like a woman spotting a lover across a crowded room. 'Most of them one star reviews. They're the most powerful.'

Harriet stared at her. She couldn't help wondering what feelings of inadequacy, hatred and jealousy drove this deluded, self-important bully.

'If you're writing the first review you can finish a book stone dead if you give it one star,' said Deborah, jabbing a podgy finger at the book shown on Harriet's computer screen.

Harriet duly gave the diet book one star, hoping desperately that she could go back later and revise it upwards. She didn't want to wreck the wretched diet book even though it didn't seem to be a terribly sensible one. She looked at Deborah and waited for her to continue. Harriet thought that the woman looked quite mad and it occurred to her that if some idiot hadn't invented the damned Internet she would have probably spent her life sending people letters and postcards written in capitals and green ink. Instead of speaking out against things that matter, the Deborahs of this world, armies of Internet trolls, attack authors not because they deserve to be attacked but because they are defenceless.

'If a book has one star no one will look at it or buy it,' Deborah said. 'And even if someone then gives it five stars it will still only have an average of three. Most books which start life with one star never recover.' She waved a hand dismissively. 'They're finished.' Harriet was appalled to see that Deborah seemed pleased by this. She clearly obtained pleasure from this prospect in the same way that young psychopaths will gain pleasure from torturing kittens or pulling the wings off flies. She leant across and peered at Harriet's computer. 'What's the title?'

Harriet told her.

'I'll give it one star too,' Deborah said. 'Then it will definitely be finished. No book ever comes back from a pair of one star reviews!' She gave Harriet another glimpse of what clearly was intended to be a smile. 'I have quite a few friends who write reviews,' she continued. 'We sometimes get together to kill off a book if we don't like the author. We call ourselves 'Satan's Little Helpers'. If one of us sees an author on television, promoting her book and looking smug and smiling too much, we'll each give it a one star rating. We try to do it quickly before there are any five star reviews. Lots of reviewers who were intending to give a book a good rating will change their minds when they see it's already got a couple of one star reviews.'

'Oh dear,' Harriet said, struggling to disguise her loathing for this woman. 'Isn't that rather cruel to the unfortunate author?'

Deborah looked at Harriet and frowned. 'You have the power,' she said. 'Why shouldn't you use it? You don't owe authors anything. It serves them right if their books are killed. It isn't personal but they shouldn't write books if they didn't expect them to be reviewed. They should grow up and learn to take it on the chin. They have to take the rough with the smooth, don't they?' Exhausted by this barrage of clichés she paused for breath. 'They're happy enough when the money is pouring into their bank accounts!'

Harriet nodded meekly, as though she understood and agreed with her. Difficult as it was she was happy to play the timid acolyte, and to listen to the woman's ravings, because she knew who would be having the last laugh.

'They do it to one another, anyway,' she said.

Harriet looked at her, puzzled.

'Authors,' she said.

'I don't understand.' Harriet really didn't know what Deborah meant.

'They write nasty reviews of other authors' books. If a book goes to the top of the bestseller lists, or appears high on a search list, it will immediately attract a clutch of one star reviews written by jealous authors anxious to downgrade a rival and make space for their own book. A book's sales can quickly be ruined if its rating goes down. And lots of authors use the system to help their own books sell more copies.'

'How on earth does that work?' Harriet asked.

'Look,' she said, as though talking to a half-witted child. 'Imagine you've written a book about...' She paused to think for a moment. 'Imagine you've written a book about eggs.'

Harriet frowned but nodded. She wondered if anyone would notice if she just beat Deborah over the head with her own laptop. She could leave her where she sat; with blood and bits of brain dribbling down her face and into her curiously decorated cup of coffee. She glanced around. She didn't think anyone would notice. The customers all had their noses stuck deep in their laptops and mobile telephones and would not have noticed an earthquake, and the staff were all busy fiddling with the coffee machine which, judging by the noise it was making, was malfunctioning in some way.

But this really wasn't the place and it certainly wasn't the time. Not yet.

'Your book on eggs is right at the top of the bestseller lists and you're doing very well. Probably making millions out of it, as all authors do.' At this point she waved a finger at me. 'You wake up one morning and when you check to see that your book is still Number One in the bestseller lists you find that someone else has also written a book about eggs.'

'That would be bad news?' suggested Harriet.

'Terrible!' said Deborah. 'You're devastated. Your competitor's book has knocked you off the top spot. You're now number two. And, worse still, when you put the words 'Eggs' into the search engine this other book comes up at the top.'

'That wouldn't be good,' Harriet agreed.

'It would be disastrous!' said Deborah. 'And to make matters worse, whereas your book has got just four stars this other book has five stars. Your book has a dozen reviews and a four star average. The newcomer's book has only been reviewed twice but both reviewers gave it the full five stars. Now, I don't know whether you know this, but readers who want a book will invariably go for the book which is most successful and which has the best reviews. If there are two books on the same subject they will almost always pick the book with the better rating.'

'I didn't know that,' Harriet said.

'Well, your competitor almost certainly knew it,' said Deborah. 'And the two five star reviews which her book has collected were probably written by her friends. If she had a decent publisher then the publisher's publicity department would have almost certainly written a dozen good reviews.'

Harriet was genuinely staggered by this. It had never occurred to either Mallory or to her that authors and publishers might try to influence the sales of a book in such an underhand way. 'Golly,' she said.

'So what do you do?'

'I don't know,' Harriet admitted.

'You write a nasty review and give your competitor's book one star. If you have a friend, you get them to give it one star too. Neither of you has to buy the book. You can just write a review and post it without seeing the book. Even if you don't have a friend you can probably knock your competitor off its perch with your review alone. If there are two five star reviews then the average review is five stars, right?'

Harriet agreed.

'But if the book has three reviews with a total of eleven stars then the average rating is under four. And so now, once again, yours is the best reviewed book on eggs.'

Harriet stared at her.

'Even if a book has four really good reviews you can bring the overall rating right down with a one star review,' she said. She cackled. Harriet had never before heard anyone else cackle but Deborah did. 'And two of you can knock a book down to three and a bit stars – pretty well killing it off permanently.'

Harriet didn't know what to say.

'So you see,' said Deborah, picking up one of her cakes and taking a huge bite out of it, 'shklptye kshe oehe gkrheer peodh bagh kwswhks shk kqt shmk!'

'I beg your pardon?' said Harriet, who hadn't understand a word.

Deborah chewed and swallowed the cake. 'Authors give one another bad reviews all the time. So they can hardly complain about readers doing it, can they?' She wagged a pudgy finger at Harriet. 'And a lot of the time they find a way to plug their own book while they're dissing another author.'

Harriet didn't understand and said so.

Deborah turned to her keyboard and played with the keys for a few moments. Harriet had to admit that Deborah was pretty adept at finding her way round the Internet and its constituent parts. 'Here you are,' she said, showing Harriet a review.

Harriet looked and could hardly believe her eyes. The writer of a cruel, one star review had shamelessly plugged another book within their review (carefully giving the full title of the recommended book).

'Do you mean that the reviewer is the author of the second book?' Harriet asked, quite shocked.

'Of course!' said Deborah. 'Authors do it all the time. They criticise a book and recommend their own book as a much better read.'

Harriet smiled weakly and sipped a little of her pineapple juice. It seemed that the world she thought she knew bore little resemblance to the world in which she was living. She turned off her laptop and closed it. She then tried not to listen as Deborah slurped her coffee and munched her way through the rest of her cake.

Chapter Three

'I'm on the first floor,' said Deborah, opening her front door. 'The ground floor flat is empty and I'm thinking of asking the landlord if I can swap. It would suit me better to be downstairs. I find the stairs a bit of a problem.'

It seemed an understatement. She was so fat that as she climbed up the stairs ahead of Harriet both her hips were brushing the walls. Another few cakes and she would, one day, find herself stuck on her own staircase. She wheezed as she climbed and had to stop and take a rest several times.

Deborah had invited Harriet back to flat when she'd expressed an interest in the 'Eggchopper', the battery powered egg-slicing device to which Deborah, the specialist one star reviewer had, in a moment of uncharacteristic weakness, awarded five stars.

'Come back with me and I'll boil and egg and show you how it works,' Deborah offered. 'I really did buy one of those things. I was so impressed that I bought a spare in case mine wore out and the company stopped making them. It's just as well I did because the company has disappeared and you can't find the Eggchopper anywhere these days. No one who has one wants to sell one. I wouldn't sell my spare for £100. Not for £200. I love hard-boiled egg sandwiches but I hate it when the eggs are crushed. I much prefer it when they're neatly sliced so that you can lay them out neatly on the bread and butter.'

'Do you try out all the things you review?' Harriet asked her, when we were still in the café. 'Do you read books, buy products and visit the places you review?'

Deborah looked at her, and leant closer and lowered her voice to a whisper. 'Not always,' she confessed. She thought for a while. 'Not often actually. Hardly ever, to be frank. But when you're an experienced reviewer you can always tell how many stars to give something – and I invariably give just the one! Reading a whole book takes far too much time. If it's a book and it's free I always download it so that I can say I'm a buyer.' She sniggered. 'I never buy books. I only ever download the ones which are offered free. There are so many free books available I can't imagine why anyone would ever buy one.'

'Do you ever review hotels, restaurants and things like theme parks?' Harriet asked. 'And do you visit any before reviewing them?'

'Yes I do review them,' Deborah said. 'But I don't have the time or the money to go to those places. Besides, if you want to be a successful reviewer you have to put in the time at the keyboard. It's the quantity that counts, you see. I try to post at least a couple of dozen reviews a day. On some days I can post fifty or more. One day last month I managed to do 100. All of them one star reviews. I have a long way to go to catch up with some of the top reviewers. The very top reviewers have done over 50,000 reviews. Some can do 300 a day.'

Harriet wondered if it ever occurred to this cruel and stupid woman that the authors of the books she was so carelessly destroying, and the businesses she was attempting to wreck, might be hurt by her cruelty.

'I go through the Internet looking for the places which I think are too expensive and I give them all one star each,' Deborah said. 'If I could give them less than one star, I would.'

Harriet nodded, as though this absurdity made sense. She realised that Deborah didn't give a damn about the authors of the books she trashed or the places she damned. If she thought of them at all it was entirely without sympathy. Indeed, she would feel thrilled if she knew that she had upset an author or made a hotel owner cry. It would make her feel even more powerful. Harriet forced herself to smile. 'You're so clever!' she told her. The lie seemed insincere but Deborah lapped it up.

And that was when Deborah invited Harriet back to her place to look at the battery powered egg-slicing machine.

'Would you like a cup of tea?' Deborah asked, when they were safely ensconced within the flat.

Harriet said that would be very nice and asked if she could use the loo first.

'It's in the bathroom,' Deborah said. Harriet didn't really need the loo but she wanted to spend a few minutes exploring the flat. She still hadn't decided how she was going to kill Deborah. The only important thing was that it needed to look like an accident. She didn't want the police asking questions. She had a lot more killing to do. And she didn't want the police looking for a serial killer. She had long ago decided that an accident, or a 'misadventure', would be best.

In the bathroom cupboard over her sink, Harriet found Deborah's stash of medication. And there, on the top shelf, in between the aspirin and a packet of Piriton, she found a bottle of nitrazepam tablets. A splendid find. Sleeping tablets. Harriet took the bottle out of the cupboard, and opened it. Her luck was in for the sleeping medicine had been prescribed as tablets and not capsules. She shook half a dozen tablets out into her hand, thought for a moment, and then added another two. Eight should be plenty. She slipped the tablets into her cardigan pocket. She then flushed the unused loo in case her hostess was paying attention, and returned to the kitchen.

'I haven't any cake but I have biscuits,' said Deborah. An open packet of chocolate digestive biscuits was standing in the middle of the table. They were clearly going to take tea there, rather than in the living room. Harriet suspected that when she wasn't watching television Deborah spent most of her time in the kitchen. There were no plates on the table. Harriet thought to herself that she would have given Deborah one star for content and presentation. This was the woman who had given one star ratings to the Ritz, the Savoy and La Caprice in London and to Le Tour d'Argent and Maxims in Paris.

Also on the table were two mugs of milky tea and an open packet of sugar. Deborah was, it seemed, too lazy to put her sugar into a bowl. There was a wet teaspoon on the table so Harriet guessed that Deborah had put sugar in her own tea. That seemed to her to be a good thing because she felt sure it would mask the taste of the sleeping tablets.

Harriet next needed to distract Deborah for a moment while she popped the tablets into her tea. She looked around. Deborah's laptop was nowhere to be seen. She was pretty sure Deborah had left it in the hallway when they'd come in. 'Can you show me some more of your reviews?'

'Of course!' Deborah replied, obviously pleased to be asked. It occurred to Harriet that if the reviews had been clumsily executed crayon drawings, Deborah would have stuck them to the fridge.

The fat reviewer tottered out to fetch the laptop and the second she'd gone Harriet emptied the pills from her cardigan pocket into Deborah's tea and gave them a good stir with the wet spoon lying on the table. She fished out a bit of fluff with the spoon and put it back into her pocket. It wasn't exactly good hygienic practice but she didn't think it mattered much since Deborah was going to be dead very soon anyway.

'I'll find you some of my favourites,' said Deborah, returning and sitting down. She took a chocolate biscuit but didn't offer the packet to Harriet. She then fired up her laptop and started messing around with it in that busy, earnest way people adopt when they're dealing with computers.

'Here you are!' she said. 'This is one of my favourites.' Harriet stood up and moved around so that she could look at the screen which was showing a review of a novel by a young woman author. The review, accompanied by a one star review, was short but not sweet. 'A rubbish book. Don't waist your money on it. Buy a packet of biscuit instead.'

The bloody woman was illiterate, thought Harriet. Deborah smiled.

'Witty, don't you think?' She took a big gulp of tea from her mug.

'Absolutely,' Harriet agreed. 'Very well put. Very clever.'

Deborah displayed half a dozen more reviews without touching her tea. And each time Harriet had to make an effort and express some interest and enthusiasm. Deborah had a debonair attitude to reviewing and seemed to believe that it was her right to publish comments and criticisms about an author's work without even taking the effort to look at the cover or read the blurb. Harriet was appalled at Deborah's behaviour but hiding her feelings was wearing her out. Her acting skills were being tested to the very limit.

Deborah seemed to have an inordinate amount of enthusiasm for the words 'It took too long to download'.

Harriet asked her about this comment (which, naturally, always accompanied a one star review).

'How do you decide that a book's taken too long?'

'Just how I feel,' Deborah replied, with a shrug. 'It varies.' She stood up, took an egg out of the refrigerator and put into a saucepan of water. She turned on the gas, lit it with a match and turned the gas up high.

'But surely it isn't the author's fault that their book takes a long time to download,' Harriet said.

'Well, I can't review the computer, can I?' she answered. 'I can only review the book.' There was a hint of temper in the reply.

It took ten minutes for Deborah to show signs of sleepiness. And another five for her eyelids to start to droop. The egg, bubbling in its pan, must have been well and truly boiled.

Harriet stood up, took her mug to the sink and emptied it. She then rinsed it out, dried it on a filthy tea-towel that had been tossed on the draining board, and then put the mug back into the cupboard from which it had been taken.

Deborah opened her eyes and looked at her. 'What are you doing?'

'Just tidying up.'

Deborah looked puzzled. She was clearly having difficulty in keeping awake.

'You wrote reviews of my husband's books,' Harriet said. She told Deborah her husband's name and the titles of some of his books.

Deborah looked at Harriet and was now even more puzzled. 'What do you mean?'

'You gave them one star each,' Harriet said. 'Do you remember?'

Deborah thought about it for a few moments and then shook her head.

Harriet found one of the reviews on the laptop. Deborah stared at it uncomprehendingly. 'So what?' she asked at last.

'You don't even remember writing any of these, do you?'

Deborah shrugged, uncaringly. Harriet wanted to hit her but didn't want to mark her. She wanted her death to look entirely natural.

'Your reviews helped push my husband over the edge,' said Harriet. 'He killed himself.'

'Not my fault if he couldn't take the criticism,' Deborah declared, belligerently.

'Of course it is,' Harriet told her. She sat down opposite the reviewer so that she could look straight at her. She pressed a few keys on the computer and closed it down.

Deborah stared at the visitor. She was now very drowsy. She tried to get up but couldn't move.

'You're going to die because of what you did,' Harriet told her.

Deborah blinked and pulled a face. 'What do you mean?'

'I drugged your tea,' said Harriet. 'I put eight sleeping tablets into it.'

Deborah sneered. 'Eight of those won't kill me,' she said defiantly.

'I know they won't. But you're going to die.'

Deborah frowned and stared. She was struggling to stay awake.

'You'll fall asleep in a couple of minutes,' Harriet told her. 'But you'll never wake up.'

'Why?' What are you going to do?' demanded Deborah, now panicking.

Harriet nodded towards the pan on the gas stove. The water was still bubbling away. 'I'm going to sit here until you're fast asleep and then I'm going to turn off the gas. Then I'm going to turn it back on but I'm not going to light it.'

'The gas?' Deborah was now genuinely afraid.

'I'll leave you to die. Your death will be reported as accidental. They'll say you took too many sleeping tablets, tried to boil an egg and forgot to light the gas.'

Deborah made one last effort to say something. Her eyes were full of fear. She knew exactly what was happening. And she knew why. Harriet felt very pleased about that.

Harriet waited another fifteen minutes until Deborah had fallen forwards onto the table and was snoring. Then she turned off the gas, poured the hot water out of the saucepan and then took the boiled egg out of the pan. She wrapped the egg in her handkerchief and put it into her pocket. She then took a second egg out of the refrigerator, put it into the saucepan and half-filled the pan with cold water. She turned the gas on but I didn't light the stove. She then picked up her bag and her coat, both of which she'd left in the hallway.

Harriet hummed a little tune to herself as she went down the stairs and let herself out into the street.

It had started to rain but she felt calm and strangely content. She wasn't euphoric, she didn't feel like skipping along the pavement or anything like that, but she felt quietly satisfied; the sort of satisfaction one feels after tackling and completing a tricky task. It never for one second occurred to her that she had done anything which others might regard as 'wrong'. She felt no more guilt than she would have done if she had killed a wasp which had just stung a loved one.

The first one had been very easy to kill. She hoped Mallory would be pleased with her. He would know that these things had to be done.

She was going to kill all of Mallory's tormentors.

Chapter Four

Harriet's husband, Mallory, had begun his working life as a reporter on a small, local newspaper in the North of England. He started out by writing down the names of people attending funerals and weddings, moved on to writing reports of council meetings and progressed to writing about local fires, burglaries, sports matches and tree planting. By the time he reached his late 30s, he had experienced all the delights of a local newspaper.

But for the last 19 years of his life he earned his living writing books.

Mallory wrote crime novels, and although he never hit the big time (there were no movie sales or million dollar three book contracts) he and Harriet had a decent standard of living. They had paid off their mortgage and never had to worry as much as some folk did about where the next meal was coming from, or whether or not they would be able to pay the house insurance or the garage bill.

In the early days, Harriet had a small income as a model and later on she worked in market research; interviewing housewives and collecting their opinions on a variety of household products. She did not find either job easy for she was a shy, rather timid woman who always found working with other people rather nerve wracking; she had drifted into these rather public occupations through chance rather than by design. People who met her, and who didn't know what she did for living, usually thought she worked in a library or some quiet office in a perenially unfashionable industry.

When she worked in modelling, Harriet was not one of those glamorous models who spent a lot of time on yachts and whose pictures appear in the papers. She was not an exceptionally beautiful woman and she didn't have a particularly voluptuous figure but she was unusually small, (a smidgeon under five feet tall) and because of her lack of size she was regularly hired to appear in magazine and newspaper advertisements for cars, aeroplanes and other products where the advertiser needed to make the viewer think there was more space than there really was. Advertising agencies promoting caravans and new houses loved her because she made the products look deceptively spacious.

Mallory's books usually received decent reviews and his work was well regarded by his publishers and his peers. On two occasions he received awards, several of his books were selected by book clubs and his books were regularly translated into two or three foreign languages.

Harriet loved her husband very much and she was immensely proud of him and what he had achieved. The nature of his death gave her deep and lasting pain and produced a lasting sense of injustice. It also aroused in her a sense of vengeance which she never previously knew existed.

All Mallory's books were published by a small family owned company run by the grandson of the founder. Mallory, who used a pen name, wrote one novel a year and he had a loyal and kind readership.

Many modern authors would probably find this strange, difficult to believe perhaps, but throughout Mallory's career he and Harriet regarded the readers as their friends. Quite a few of his readers sent the couple Christmas cards and even small gifts. Mallory always used to enjoy the mail the readers sent and he invariably found that any suggestions and corrections were put kindly and meant well.

During the early and middle years of his career, Mallory's books always sold between 5,000 and 8,000 copies in hardback in the UK, and three times that in paperback. In the days when public libraries had decent budgets (and didn't spend all their money on DVDs and coffee machines) his books were enormously popular with library users. His backlist sold well too and when you add in the income from translation rights, occasional audio and large print rights and various other bits and pieces you can see why he and Harriet were never rich but always comfortable.

These sales figures would not impress those authors who dominate the bestseller lists but, as Harriet's father always said, in a not unkindly way, not everyone in the race can win a cup. Mallory enjoyed writing his books and the readers enjoyed reading them; the publishers made money and Mallory's advances and royalties were enough for the two of them to live on. No one was getting rich, but everyone was happy.

Suddenly, almost overnight, things went wrong and their world fell apart. And thanks to the Internet, the readers who had been cherished friends became their deadly enemies.

The problems began when the publishing company with which Mallory had been closely associated for many years was sold to a conglomerate and the editor, who had worked with Mallory for most of his career, decided to retire and take his pension. The editor told Mallory that the sale of his small, semi-detached house in a rather dirty London suburb would enable him to purchase a decent sized country cottage with six acres and a stream; leaving enough left over to ensure that he could deal with most fiscal emergencies. He would, he told them, have loved to have continued working but he didn't fit in with the new company's requirements.

A new editor called Fiona was appointed to look after Mallory's books.

Fiona was 22-years-old and six months out of university. Her mother was a favoured cousin of the chairman of the conglomerate which had bought Mallory's publishers. Fiona admitted, without shame or embarrassment, that she had not read any of Mallory's books and she showed absolutely no interest in them. On the sole occasion when they met, she told him that he was too old to be writing books and that his books were too old-fashioned to attract any readers.

'You've had your time,' she said, making it clear that as far as she was concerned he had had his chance and was a proven failure. She said that she was keen to find young authors whom the company could promote and that Mallory's readers were too old and were dying off rapidly. She even attacked Mallory for not being able to send his work to her as an email attachment and said that she thought he was a dinosaur for not having an email address.

Three days after Mallory delivered his latest book Fiona rejected it by telephone, telling him that although there was 'nothing wrong with the book per se', she didn't think that the book was what the company was looking for and that she had, therefore, decided to 'allow' him to offer it to other publishing houses. She wished him luck with it and said that in view of his long history with the company she would not demand repayment of the first third of his advance which had already been paid. (It was the company's policy to pay authors one third of their advance when they signed their contract, one third on the delivery of the manuscript and one third when the book was published.) She added that they did not intend to keep any of his previous books in print and that they were, indeed, selling the existing stock of books to a remainder merchant so that they could be sold off cheaply in cut price stores. 'The rights in your books will, of course, revert to you and you will be free to offer the books to another publisher,' she said, making it pretty clear that she thought that was about as likely as her waking up to find that Mallory had been awarded the Nobel Prize for Literature.

Mallory was broken by that call. His self-confidence was destroyed and for a month he didn't do anything apart from mope about the house and the garden. He didn't write a word. This was unusual for him. Harriet couldn't remember when he hadn't spent at least part of each day working on his next book. Now he just sat on a bench in the garden for hours at a time, staring unseeing at a large oak tree as though expecting it to start dancing a jig or burst into song.

Eventually, Harriet managed to persuade Mallory to try some other publishers.

He printed out half a dozen copies of the first chapter of his most recent book and sent them, together with a three-page outline, a typically modest CV and a short, introductory letter to editorial directors at a number of publishing houses. He even enclosed enough stamps to cover the return postage in the naïve belief that this would ensure that he received replies.

You might imagine that since he had been working in the world of publishing for many decades Mallory would have made friends in the business, but he was shy, quietly spoken and rather deaf and he was not a sociable man. He was not what is popularly known as a 'networker' and he did not have a little black book full of the names and addresses of useful contacts.

Four months later just two of the publishers had bothered to send a reply.

One reply came from an editorial assistant who suggested that Mallory should consult the *Writers' and Artists' Yearbook* to find a literary agent if he wanted to become a published author.

The second reply, included in with a packet containing the material he had posted out, consisted of an unsigned 'with compliments' slip across which someone had scribbled 'we don't consider unsolicited manuscripts'.

The other four editorial directors ignored Mallory's letter completely, and, he assumed, kept the stamps he had enclosed.

Mallory had never used a literary agent. He had stayed with the same publisher all his writing life and the rights department there had always handled translation rights for his books. Any money he had earned on top of his usual advance and royalties had simply been added to his six monthly royalty cheque. He was a loyal and relatively unambitious man and he had never seen the need for someone to stand between him and his publisher.

But when the young, new editor made it clear that she didn't want his books, and the publishers refused to consider his latest typescript, it seemed that Mallory would have to try to find an agent.

The blunt truth was that he and Harriet needed an income. He was too young to retire (he didn't have one of those nice, inflation-linked pensions civil servants enjoy and they had very little money in their small, private pension fund) and he didn't know what else he would do with his life if he had to give up writing books.

The newspaper he had once worked for had long since closed down and it didn't take much research to show that his chances of earning a living writing freelance articles were pretty well non-existent. The world was, it seemed, pretty well stocked with would-be writers who were prepared to sell their work for little more than the cost of the electricity required to email it to an editor.

Harriet's income, which had never been great enough to keep them, had fallen off in recent years and was now non-existent. The modelling agencies and the market research companies all wanted younger, prettier women. It seemed that the motor car, aeroplane and new home advertisers had found a new generation of under-sized women to help emphasise the spaciousness of their products.

And so off went another pile of letters – with yet more stamps pinned to them. Mallory wrote to dozens of different agencies. He wrote to the big, successful ones, the medium sized ones and the ones which seemed to consist of a man or a woman working from a spare bedroom, or a converted garage. There seemed to be quite a lot of those.

Most of the agents didn't bother to reply. They just kept the stamps. The few agents who did make the effort to send replies all found different ways to say much the same thing. They told Mallory that he was too old, that there was no longer any clear market for his books and that it was clear that his time had come and gone. Actually, they weren't always that polite.

Harriet and Mallory had, it seemed, both become redundant. And it was at this moment that Harriet thought they had reached the low point of their lives. How wrong she was.

The pair took their first step down into what would turn out to be their own personal version of hell as a result of a weekend they spent with a friend Dora and her husband.

Dora, who used to work for a large publishing company, and had herself been given the opportunity to explore new employment possibilities, had put together what she called a 'portfolio' of jobs in media consulting. Leonard, her husband, worked as an IT consultant.

It was during that weekend that Mallory and Harriet discovered the world of eBooks. It was that discovery which led directly to Mallory's death.

They had both heard of eBooks, of course. But they were not 'computer literate' people and they had both grown up in a world where the cutting edge of information technology was represented by alphabet soup.

Mallory had a computer, of course, but he used an old-fashioned word processing programme which he had favoured for years. It seemed to work well for him and it rarely broke down. He'd learned all its little ways and felt comfortable with it, just as he had once felt comfortable with his old typewriter and its own little idiosyncrasies.

Neither of them had ever felt the need to connect to the World Wide Web, to email people, to publish photographs of themselves having a barbecue or posing naked. Neither of them had even tried Internet shopping. The people working at Mallory's publisher had computers with access to the Internet but they had never put any pressure on Mallory to move into their world. They had some clever equipment which somehow managed to turn what he'd written on his old-fashioned software into something their computers could read.

Mallory used to laugh about the number of emails they all sent to one another. He always used to say that people in offices used to get through their work much faster when they didn't spend half the day talking about what they'd done yesterday and the other half talking about what they were going to do tomorrow. He didn't have any time for texting, either. He thought people did far more than enough of that; wasting great chunks of their lives on silly bits of gossip.

Harriet told Leonard and Dora what had happened to Mallory. They had always been great fans and Mallory always sent them a signed copy of every new book he had published. The publishers used to send Mallory six copies of every book he wrote and Leonard and Dora always got one of the six.

Leonard was absolutely flabbergasted. Dora was too. They said that they thought Mallory had been treated very badly and they were even more shocked when he told them that he couldn't find a new publisher, or even an agent to represent him.

'I always thought your publishers were daft to make their paperbacks so damned big,' said Dora. 'Most people want fairly light paperbacks that are easy to put into a pocket or handbag. That's why they buy them. They want something to read on the train or on holiday or in bed. But for some reason best known to themselves your publishers, like lots of others, made their paperbacks bigger and bigger. Eventually they were making paperbacks so big that it became impossible for anyone going on holiday to take more than one book with them. The eBook reader is proving popular because it enables people to take a whole library of books away with them on holiday.'

'And the bigger books cost more to post!' pointed out Leonard. 'I bet the people selling books by mail order have really suffered as books have got heavier.'

'Publishers couldn't have committed commercial suicide more effectively if they'd tried,' said Dora.

'Have you thought about publishing your books yourself?' asked Leonard. 'You could cut out the publishers completely and keep everything you earn for yourselves.'

Mallory said he wasn't keen on that. He said he thought he was too old to be carrying books around to the bookshops and too poor to pay all the print costs.

Leonard laughed and explained that no one actually printed books these days. He said that bookshops and printers were going out of business faster than record shops and vinyl pressing companies and that it was dead easy to publish your own book for next to nothing by using the Internet. He fetched his laptop, opened it up and showed them all the eBooks that were available. Mallory and Harriet were flabbergasted. Just about every well-known author in the world was there. Leonard actually bought an eBook to show them just how easy it was.

'Take a look and see if any of Mallory's books are on sale,' suggested Dora.

So Leonard pressed a few more keys and a few moments later several pages full of Mallory's books appeared. Most of his early books were there (though not as eBooks, of course) and Harriet and Mallory were shocked to see that people could buy almost any of them for a penny each. It was no wonder that his (and everyone else's) backlist sales had collapsed.

In the bad old days, readers who wanted to find a backlist book by an author they liked would either have to trawl through scores of second hand bookshops or else order a new copy from a bookshop. Mallory and Harriet discovered to their astonishment (and horror) that it was now possible to pick up a copy of almost any old book for a penny.

'How can people make money selling books for a penny?' demanded Mallory.

Leonard explained that the sellers made their money out of the extra they charged for postage and packing. He said the amount of competition on the Web meant that books, like just about everything else, sold for the lowest possible prices. 'Huge numbers of books now sell for a penny,' he explained. 'The people selling them make 10 or 20 pence profit on each sale as long as the fixed fee they're allowed to charge for postage is slightly higher than the real cost of posting a book.'

'It seems like a hard way to make a living,' Mallory said. 'Lugging all those books to the Post Office for a few pennies profit.'

'Most of the people selling books are amateurs,' explained Leonard. 'They sell books as a bit of a side line. They're just trying to make a few extra pounds a week for a bit of work they can do in the evenings and at weekends. And, of course, most of them don't pay any income tax on their extra earnings.' He shrugged and grinned. 'But none of that has to bother you,' he went on. 'If you publish your own books as eBooks then all you have to do is make sure that you sell them reasonably cheaply. You don't have to wrap up the books you're selling. You have no print costs, no storage costs and no postage costs. You don't even need a proper office.' As a rider to all this enthusiasm he did add that Mallory would probably need to find someone prepared to help turn his books into eBooks.

'You've got some reviews already!' Dora told Mallory. She pointed out that one of Mallory's early books had four yellow stars alongside it and explained that readers of a book could write their review and have it printed alongside the book's details. She pressed a key and the reviews appeared on the screen. They weren't at all bad. One of them was a bit sniffy, complaining that one of Mallory's characters didn't behave consistently, but the rest were pretty complimentary.

Both Mallory and Harriet were much cheered by what they had learned; they felt that they had found the future and that it was not, perhaps, quite as frightening as they had feared it would be.

Dora told them that a third of all the books published are published by their authors and that self-published books now make up nearly a half of all the books which are sold.

When Mallory expressed surprise at this, Dora explained that self-published authors have huge advantages over traditional publishing companies. They can charge much less for their books because big companies have huge in-house costs and invariably need to protect the sales of their printed books.

'Publishers have lost touch,' said Dora. 'They're too slow and their overheads are too high. No author needs an outside publisher these days. Agents, publishers, bookshops, wholesalers and printers are all living on borrowed time.'

Mallory and Harriet had no idea just how badly they had been misled, and lulled into a false sense of security, by those few, kindly reviews. They did not realise that these kind and sensitive reviews had been written by Mallory's regular, long-term readers: people who had read and enjoyed his work for many years.

Chapter Five

To begin with, Mallory was excited by the prospect of being able to republish his books in eBook format. He found a young man who helped turn the books into eBooks, and those of his long-term fans who had graduated to the world of the Internet and the electronic book welcomed his new adventure and greeted the availability of his books for this new format with unexpected but welcome enthusiasm.

It looked, for a while, as though they had found the answer to Mallory's publishing prayers.

And then things started to go wrong. And new readers started to write their reviews.

One reviewer gave a book a one star review because it had taken a long time to download. A second gave the same book one star because he or she didn't like the cover. A third gave a book one star because he suspected that the book didn't contain enough violence. He boasted that because of this suspicion he hadn't actually bothered to read the book. A fourth said that the book seemed old-fashioned (it was set in the 1930s) and so he also gave it one star. 'Don't bother. Watch the TV instead.'

Within less than a day, a book which had had four and a half stars had two and a half stars. And the book stopped selling. No one buys eBooks which have less than three stars.

'The bad reviews are part and parcel of the game these days,' said someone they knew. 'You have to suck it up. Don't take it personally.' It seemed a cruel thing to say and it certainly didn't make Mallory feel any better. He always worked hard on his books and put his heart and soul into them, so of course he took unjust criticism very personally. How could it be impersonal?

And neither he nor Harriet could stop looking at the reviews.

As the sales of Mallory's books continued to drop they both found themselves looking at the star ratings on an almost hourly basis. And once they'd looked at the star ratings they both found themselves looking at the individual reviews.

Mallory became increasingly upset by them. He would have probably been able to accept the reviews if they had been fair. If readers had written bad reviews because they didn't like his books it would have been difficult but it would have been understandable. Not every author can please every reader.

But a high proportion of the reviews were cruel and entirely unjustifiable and Mallory, who had always been a sensitive man, found himself struggling to cope.

For a while he tried to ignore the reviews; to pretend that they weren't there at all.

He confined himself to checking to see how many books had been sold and what he'd earned.

But that didn't work.

Whenever a book's sales slumped still further he couldn't resist looking to see what had happened. And it was always a result of another one star review; too often patronising and dismissive, too often unintelligently written, too often unjust or wildly inaccurate, too often cruel for the sake of being cruel.

In the old days, if an inaccurate, unfair, libellous or spiteful review was published in a newspaper or magazine, an author could write to the editor and both defend himself and correct errors. The writer could defend himself; he had rights and a voice.

But with the Internet that isn't the way things work. The libel, the inaccurate abuse, remains there forever.

After two weeks of the acutest distress, Mallory went to see his doctor. Harriet went with him. The regular man was away on a course and Mallory saw a young girl just out of medical school. She didn't seem to understand, or to care terribly much, about his situation. She simply gave him a prescription for a drug called Prozac which she said would help.

Shortly after starting the pills, Mallory waited until Harriet went out to the corner shop to buy some groceries and then, in her absence, he took all his Prozac medicine, together with every other pill they had in the medicine cabinet.

The paramedics did everything they could but although they rushed Mallory to hospital, the doctors could not save him.

Mallory and Harriet had been married for over 30 years and had rarely been separated for more than a few hours. Mallory was Harriet's whole life and when he died she felt as though she had died too. She felt that the Internet's one star reviewers had killed her husband as surely as if they had attacked him physically.

At first Harriet wanted to die too.

It wasn't until after the funeral that she realised exactly what she had to do, both to exact revenge for her beloved husband and to protect other authors who might find themselves in a similar situation.

Chapter Six

After she had silenced Deborah, Harriet found it difficult to decide which reviewer to deal with next. So, to make things simple, she put the names of a dozen reviewers into one of Mallory's old hats and picked out a name at random.

The lucky (or, rather, unlucky) winner of this impromptu selection process was a man called Max – though that was not, of course, the name he used on the Internet.

Like many other critics, Max had coyly hidden himself behind a pseudonym which he clearly believed would allow him to sneer and abuse without any responsibility or retribution.

But he had done very little to protect his identity, and his arrogance and carelessness meant that Harriet succeeded in identifying him within just a couple of hours.

It occurred to her that if she, a complete novice in these matters, could identify reviewers in such a short space of time then an experienced computer user would surely be able to identify reviewers in a much shorter time period. Harriet concluded that anyone who keys in their real address and real credit card details and then thinks that they can hide behind an Internet pseudonym is naïve and is asking to be unmasked and punished.

Max turned out to be considerably older than Harriet had expected.

His reviews made him sound pompous, supercilious, patronising and something of a pseudointellectual and so, naturally, she had assumed that he was probably still in his teens.

However, although he still dressed and lived like a student, Max was actually well into his mid-forties. Harriet was greatly relieved by this because she had begun to feel some misgivings about killing a youth who might conceivably grow out of his adolescent behaviour.

But Max wasn't going to grow out of anything. He'd clearly done all the growing up he was going to do.

Although he liked to describe himself as a polymath (on his Facebook page he boasted that he had edited 500 Wikipedia profiles and that he was a qualified computer specialist, economist, historian and literary critic) Max had never enjoyed the delights of gainful employment. He had left school at the age of 16 with no qualifications, other than a piece of paper confirming that he had some rudimentary carpentry skills, and for over a quarter of a century he had been nothing more than a constant drain on the national economy. He was one of those people about whom politicians are talking on those rare occasions when they dare to speak about the burden created by the work-shy, long-term unemployed.

Despite his claims to be a polymath, Max was barely literate and although he had some basic computer skills it should alarm websites such as Wikipedia to know that such a man was writing and editing material regarded by the culturally innocent as useful and reliable.

The one subject upon which Max could really claim to be an expert was Britain's State benefit system, and in order to maximise his income he had, it is fair to say, become something of an authority on the subject of malingering. He had genuine heart trouble but before the cardiac problem had become apparent he had successfully convinced many doctors and benefits officials that he was a chronic back pain sufferer and a victim of a wide variety of stress-related disorders.

Max lived in a squalid, run down two bedroomed home on a council estate in a Glasgow suburb and was, Harriet quickly learned, heartily disliked by his neighbours. Local children used to throw refuse at him and he had 'repaired' his broken ground floor windows with sheets of rusty, corrugated iron.

Harriet managed to find all this out by going door to door in his neighbourhood and posing as a market researcher.

She had worked in this field earlier in her life (when her modelling career stumbled to a halt) and knew that most people are surprisingly willing to share private and confidential information with complete strangers.

If you knock on their door with a smile on your face and a clipboard in your hand, two out of three householders will tell you whatever you want to know. Out on the street a clipboard makes the holder disappear; to become as invisible as the postman. You can ask people what washing powder they prefer, how much money they make and how often they have sex. Harriet always found that if you start with the boring questions and gently move towards the more intimate ones you can ask people anything you like. Lots of people have no opportunity to talk about themselves and so they welcome the chance to do so. Talking to a stranger makes it even easier, of course, because you don't have to worry about the consequences. Harriet always remained totally non-judgemental and found that this helped enormously.

Harriet knew, from talking to friends who were still involved in the marketing world, that despite the popularity of social media websites it has become even easier to obtain information this way. Maybe this is because a surprising number of people are genuinely lonely and crave real human contact.

If you dress reasonably smartly (so that people don't think you're going to beg, steal or try to con them into making a monthly donation to Greenpeace), and you carry a smart looking clipboard with a few forms fastened to it so that you look 'official' (but not so official that folk worry you're from the local council) a surprising number of people will answer almost any questions the clipboard holder likes to ask.

Harriet bought a brightly coloured clipboard from a local stationer and to it she clipped a couple of dozen forms she'd composed and printed out. She then picked 30 or 40 houses close to Max's home and slowly worked her way round the neighbourhood.

She told everyone who answered their door that she was doing market research for a company (which, she said, she wasn't allowed to name) which was investigating people's attitudes towards their neighbours. And when she steered the conversation in the right direction, she soon found herself collecting information and opinions about Max.

Every neighbourhood in the world has a difficult resident, someone who doesn't make any effort to get on with his or her neighbours, someone anti-social who has annoying habits and attitudes. And it quickly became apparent that Max was the legendary neighbour from hell. No one liked him. He was arrogant and self-satisfied, supercilious and sneery. He would bully young children but like all bullies he was a coward at heart and would quickly shy away when confronted by the tougher looking adult residents. He would shout abuse at the elderly, and had on at least one occasion pushed a man from his wheelchair.

Even on a fairly rough housing estate, where a large proportion of the population was unemployed and an almost equally large proportion had criminal records, Max was marked out as an unusually unpleasant character; generally regarded as greedy, grasping and lazy. He was a troublemaker and a liar and cheat. He was a loner but he had a reputation as a sexual predator. Three women told Harriet that he had asked them for sex. One had told her husband who had given Max a good beating. One woman, who admitted that she was a part-time prostitute, told Harriet that she found Max such a repulsive individual that she would not have sex with him even though he had offered her money. She laughed and admitted that she'd never turned down any other customer.

Max was a heavy smoker and he seemed to live on a diet of fish and chips, pie and chips and fish and chips again. One of the women who had been approached by Max said she'd heard that he'd had a couple of minor heart attacks.

Just in case anyone ever asked questions about her, Harriet disguised herself a little while conducting her interviews.

She wore a black, shoulder length wig, a pair of those cheap reading glasses you can buy from supermarkets (the least powerful she could find), rather too much make up and a pair of four inch heels which made her seem considerably taller. She didn't expect anyone to ask questions about her but it seemed silly to take chances when there was absolutely no need to do so.

She found out a good deal about Max and his habits.

It seemed to her that it would be reckless to try to kill someone without knowing a good deal about them. Some people might feel that if you are going to kill someone then you owe it to them, out of respect, to study them carefully. Harriet didn't think that way at all. Her only reason for doing her research was that it would ensure that she could kill the wretched man without putting herself at risk.

Her careful study of Deborah's habits had proved invaluable.

And so Harriet found out where Max shopped and, most important of all, she found out where he spent his evenings.

Once Harriet had done all her research she knew exactly what she was going to do.

She took a train to Birmingham, rented a room in a small hotel near to the station and spent an awful evening at a nightclub in the city centre. The club was so poorly lit that it was almost impossible to see anything and so noisy that it was almost impossible to hear any conversation. There was no floor show and no live music; just a long bar and a man on a podium playing recorded music.

But Harriet wasn't there to have a good time and she had absolutely no difficulty in buying the drugs she needed.

She just asked at the bar; asked the barman to point out the local pusher.

To begin with the barman pretended not to know what she was talking about. However, when Harriet gave him a £10 note, he directed her to a spot where two teenage boys were doing a roaring trade selling stuff from a rather scruffy backpack.

Harriet told the boys she wanted some Viagra. At first they offered her tablets but when she insisted that she needed the capsules they quickly found a supply of those. She also bought some amyl nitrate ampoules and a dozen Rohypnol sleeping tablets. She wasn't sure that she'd need the Rohypnol, a powerful benzodiazepine, but thought she'd buy some since they were so readily available.

The boys had an enormous supply of drugs; all boxed in small, airtight, Tupperware sandwich containers which were neatly labelled in fluorescent ink that shone in the dark. It was all very efficient. The boys clearly didn't give a damn why Harriet needed the drugs or what she intended to do with them. All they were interested in was the cash she handed over. The whole transaction took place in the dark of the nightclub and so there was no evidence at all to tie her into the purchase of the drugs. Harriet had got into the habit of paying cash for everything; especially hotel bills and railway tickets.

She left the nightclub immediately after buying the drugs and went back to her impersonal, cheap hotel room, where she needed to make some minor adjustments to one of the products she'd bought. Planning a murder was something she was surprisingly good at. When Mallory was alive she often used to help him with research for his thrillers. He always needed to find new ways for one character to kill another and Harriet enjoyed working with him and working alone; staying in the background, suited her perfectly.

Chapter Seven

Harriet managed to meet Max in a scruffy, down at heel public bar at one of the three public houses he frequented. Max was what Mallory used to call a 'professional drinker'. He didn't go to the pub to meet friends, to play pool or darts or to chat to the landlord or barmaid; he went to the pub to drink. And the pub he frequented most commonly was one of those down at heel boozers where it is almost as cheap to drink alcohol as it would be to buy booze in the local supermarket and drink it at home.

The pub was a dreary looking place which had last been painted sometime in the 1960s. It looked as if it were waiting to be demolished and turned into a small supermarket or a fast food restaurant. It wasn't big enough, or in the right area, to be bought by a brewery and upgraded.

Harriet knew which pub Max was in because she'd followed him from his home. It wasn't difficult. He was so unaware of his surroundings that she could have followed him in a Centurion tank and he still wouldn't have spotted her.

She was wearing much the same disguise she'd worn for her marketing research, though instead of a clipboard she was now carrying a grey nylon laptop bag with a shoulder strap. She needed a prop as an excuse to meet Max and the computer seemed appropriate. The only difference in her attire was that she was wearing a shorter skirt.

Once she'd seen him go into his pub Harriet walked to another nearby public house, went into the lounge bar and ordered a sandwich and a lemonade. She wanted Max to have a few drinks inside him before they met. She wanted him to be slightly drunk, eager and unquestioning. And she didn't want to have to spend the whole evening in his company. She made the sandwich last as long as she could and then sat in a corner reading a copy of one of Mallory's paperbacks. After her husband's death, Harriet had started re-reading all his books. She thought them very well-written, with strong characters and well-crafted plots. Reading the books made her feel connected to him; as though he were still alive.

At half past nine she closed her book, put it into her bag and left. She then walked the short distance to the pub where Max was drinking.

The bar was almost empty.

Two old men were sitting in one corner sipping pints of Guinness. And Max was sitting in another corner reading a newspaper. He had the remains of a pint of bitter in front of him. Between Max and the two old men there was a gas fire. Someone, presumably the landlord, had lit it but kept it turned very low. The landlord, a red-faced, glum looking fellow who had clearly eaten too many of his own pies and probably drunk too much of his own beer, served Harriet a tonic water and then turned back to the racing page of one of the tabloids. He looked as if he needed a good bath and an hour with a scrubbing brush. His shirt and threadbare jumper were both filthy and he stank. He had to be the landlord. No employee would dare turn up for work in such a state.

Harriet chose a table about two yards away from Max, put down her drink and immediately took out her laptop. The two old men didn't give any sign that they had even noticed her enter. They both just stared into space, as though they were lost in thought or, perhaps, just too stupid to have any interest in what was going on around them. Max, however, did notice Harriet and he didn't stop noticing her. Even when he went to the bar to refill his glass he kept his eyes on her, mostly on her legs.

Once she'd switched on her computer Harriet concentrated hard, as though typing something, and for the next ten minutes or so she tried to give the impression that she was working. It's easy to look as if you're busy when you've got a computer opened, switched on and lit up. After continuing with this charade for a while she leant back, shook her head and glowered at the screen as though in despair. She then took a large gulp of her tonic water (which she hoped Max would think was laced with vodka), tapped a few keys again and then banged the table with her fist.

'Having trouble?' Max asked, responding as she had hoped. He might as well have been one of Pavlov's dogs. He got up, picked up his drink, moved across to her table and sat down beside her without bothering to ask if she minded. It occurred to her that she really hadn't needed to bring the laptop at all. All she had to do was sit in the pub and Max would have tried to pick her up. She wasn't flattering herself. He'd have tried to pick up any woman.

'Damned computer,' she said, picking up the laptop and putting it back into its grey bag. 'I've been working round here and was supposed to email a report to my boss but I can't get the damned thing to work properly.'

'There's no Wi-Fi here,' said Max. 'And the reception is dead dodgy, you know what I mean?'

'Well he'll just have to wait until tomorrow,' Harriet said. 'I need a bit of a break anyway.' She sipped at the remains of her drink.

'I've got one of those things,' Max said. 'Mine is a Toshiba.' He tried to remember something else about it but couldn't. 'Japanese,' he added rather lamely.

Harriet looked interested.

'I write stuff myself,' he told me. 'Reviews.'

She tried to look impressed.

'Dead easy when you've got the hang of it. You can get free books now. Did you know that?'

Harriet said she didn't.

'I'll show you how to do it if you like,' he offered. 'You can download as many as you like. Completely free.'

'Do you read a good deal?' she asked him.

'Not so much,' he admitted. 'To be honest, I've never found a book yet that I could get into. Films are more my cup of tea. Books are a bit slow.'

'But you write reviews of them?'

'Oh yeah! You don't have to read them to review them. You can tell after a page or so whether they're going to be any good. Most of these authors don't know what they're doing. They deserve a bit of a kicking. Put them in their place, eh?' He grinned.

'You're a hard man,' Harriet said, not meaning the double entendre.

'You better believe it!' he laughed. He winked. 'Do you want another one of those?' he asked, standing. 'What is it? Vodka?'

'Oh I'd better just have tonic,' she said. 'I'm already feeling a bit squiffy. I don't drink much.'

He grinned and wandered off to the bar. She watched as the barman pulled him another pint and then made her a double vodka and tonic. She wasn't surprised but was glad her previous drink had been plain tonic water.

'There you are,' said Max, putting the drink down in front of her. 'I put a little something in it. Help get you in the mood.' He sniggered. 'Do you know what I mean?'

'Oh you really shouldn't have,' she told him. But she picked up the glass and took a sip. 'If I drink all this you'll have to carry me home.'

'No problem,' he said, with a leer. 'Where are you staying?'

She told him the name of a hotel in the nearby town. It wasn't the hotel where she was booked in.

'What's your name?'

'Sam,' lied Harriet.

'You don't look like a bloke!' he laughed, as though amused by his own wit. 'Do you know what I mean?' He looked down at her chest and winked lasciviously.

Harriet tried to laugh at his little pleasantry. Her laugh didn't sound very convincing to her but Max seemed happy enough.

'I'm thinking of having a tattoo done,' he told her. 'On my arm.' He patted his left biceps. 'Do you know what I mean?' He leant closer and she could smell the beer on his breath. It wasn't all she could smell. She wondered how long it had been since he'd had a shower. It was a toss up whether he or the pub's landlord smelt worse.

'I saw picture of the one I want,' he said. 'A wolf with its teeth bared. Snarling. Do you know what I mean?'

'That would be wonderful,' she said, wondering why no one else had killed him.

'I've got a picture of it in my flat, do you know what I mean,' he said. It was clear now that what sounded like a question wasn't a question at all. He was such a sad, pathetic creature that for a moment she actually came to close to feeling sorry for him. And then she remembered the semi-literate condemnations he had written of Mallory's books. He'd written three reviews. 'Boring. Got it for free and felt cheeted.'. 'Not enough vilence.' 'Not worth what I paid for it and I got it for free.' Those were the three reviews. She remembered Mallory's face when he'd read them. All written on the same damned day. Mallory had been a strong man but he'd cried when he'd read those reviews and they had probably been the comments which had finally destroyed his hope. Like all one star reviewers, Max had clearly never written anything more than a single sentence review. Now that she'd met him, Harriet very much doubted if he'd ever even read any book.

Max put an arm around Harriet and she tried not to flinch. She needed him to think that she found him attractive. He tried to smile but just ended up showing a mouthful of stained and half-rotten teeth. He seemed very pleased with himself, and full of expectation.

He was, she thought, like a passenger on the Titanic ten minutes before the collision with the iceberg. Everything seemed to be going so well, but the future wasn't going to be quite as much fun as he clearly expected it to be.

'Do you like tattoos?' he asked. He clearly did not have a wide range of conversational subjects.

'I've not really thought about it,' she replied. She took another sip of her vodka and tonic. 'You shouldn't have bought me this,' she told him. 'I get tiddly very easily.'

'Nothing wrong with being tiddly,' he laughed. 'Help you relax and enjoy yourself. Do you know what I mean?' He put a hand on her leg and slid it up her thigh.

'Not here,' she whispered.

He kissed her.

It was the moment she'd been dreading. She'd known it was coming but she'd been dreading it. He tasted foul. She pushed him away. 'Not in here,' she repeated.

'Come back to my place then,' he said. 'It's not far. I'll show you the picture of that tattoo I'm going to have done.' He actually leered. 'I've got some great porn, too. Do you like porn?'

Harriet played the modest virgin and pretended to think about his invitation. 'We've only just met,' she protested.

He suddenly squeezed one of her breasts hard, as though he were pressing one of those old-fashioned motor car horns. He seemed to think she would like it, and be excited by it. She jumped and knocked his hand away. He laughed and squeezed her other breast.

'You're too damned randy!' she said.

'I'll give you a good time,' he promised. He finished his beer, then burped and winked again. 'Do you know what I mean?'

Harriet put her hand on his thigh and leant closer to him. 'I've got some Viagra. They're double strength. Help you keep it up all night.' She took a deep breath and slid her hand up to the top of his thigh.

He moved her hand even further up his thigh and then put his hand on top of hers to stop her moving it away. 'Feel that, I don't need pills!' he said. He laughed. 'Randy bitch aren't you?'

'One of these will make it a night neither of us will forget,' she told him. She wriggled her hand from under his, reached down into her computer bag and took out the piece of tissue in which she'd wrapped the doctored Viagra. She unwrapped the capsule and held it out to him. 'Take it now,' she told him. 'By the time we get back to your place it will have started working.'

He looked at it and seemed reluctant. 'I'm on pills for my heart, do you know what I mean? Do you think this will be OK?'

'Of course it will!' she promised. 'You'll be up for hours. Bigger and stronger than ever.'

'I don't need no capsule to give you a good seeing to,' he protested. As well as being an expert in the use of the double negative, he was clearly one of the last great romantics.

'You need this one,' she told him.

He popped the capsule into his mouth and washed it down with the dregs in his beer glass.

Harriet toyed with her glass, sipping at it. The pill would work in less than an hour. She wanted him to start feeling the effects of it before they got back to his flat. She put her glass down and squeezed his thigh. For the next twenty minutes or so he told her what he was going to do to her, in great detail. Harriet bravely resisted the temptation to tell him what she was going to do to him.

'Come on then,' she said, having looked at her watch. She stood and picked up her computer bag. 'Let's get back to your place before the capsule starts to work.'

She walked briskly out of the pub and he followed her, trotting behind like a faithful puppy. Outside he caught up with her and put his arm around her. Harriet could feel her heart beating fast and hoped his was too. The Viagra capsule he had taken contained the contents of all the capsules she'd purchased in Birmingham. Just one capsule would have put his heart under strain; he'd taken the active ingredients from six capsules – enough to put even the healthiest of hearts under pressure. Moreover, Max did not have a healthy heart and he'd taken the capsules on top of several pints of beer. He lowered his arm and clutched her buttock. He was not a subtle man. 'I like women with plenty of meat on them,' he told her. 'Do you know what I mean?' It wasn't difficult to see why the local women kept well away from him. Harriet wondered how long it had been since he'd actually had a lucky evening. 'Your arse isn't bad,' he added in what she assumed he intended as some sort of consolation compliment. He gave it another squeeze. She desperately wanted to knee him in the balls but she stayed patient and did nothing.

They walked on for half a mile or so. The pavement was deserted. Occasionally, he squeezed one part of her or another. Occasionally, he murmured what he obviously thought were provocative endearments but which largely consisted of obscene and rather violent threats.

And then he started to walk a little more slowly.

'Hurry up,' Harriet whispered, as though eager for him to turn his words into actions.

'I'm feeling a bit dizzy,' he complained. 'I can't see properly. And I've got a bloody awful headache. Do you know what I mean?'

'You're just over excited,' she told him.

'My heart feels as though it's going to burst out of my chest.' He stopped, bent forwards and put his hands on his knees. Even in the dark of the evening Harriet could see that he didn't look well. He was pale and sweating.

'Are you OK?' Harriet asked. Max didn't speak. She put her hand into her computer bag and found the amyl nitrate ampoules. They were made of thin glass. She broke one of the capsules and held it under his nose.

'What the hell is that?' he asked, jerking back his head.

'It's for your heart,' she told him. In a way she was being honest. The amyl nitrate was intended to have an effect on his heart. But, sadly for him, not a good effect. Amyl nitrate, Viagra and alcohol are a dangerous and explosive combination. Taken together they will kill a healthy man, let alone a man with a bad heart. She broke a second amyl nitrate capsule.

'How's that?' she asked.

Max was clutching his chest. 'No better,' he managed to murmur.

She broke two more of the glass capsules and held them under his nose. He was now clearly in considerable pain. She wrapped the pieces of thin glass in a paper tissue and put them in her pocket. 'Do you want me to call a doctor?'

'Call an ambulance!'

'Is it bad?'

For a moment he didn't say anything. He couldn't say anything. 'Ambulance!' he managed at last.

'I don't think I will,' Harriet said flatly, without emotion.

Max was now sitting on the pavement, staring up at her. He was in terrible pain but he was also clearly puzzled. Harriet felt nothing but contempt for him.

'Did you enjoy writing reviews?' she asked.

He stared at her, puzzled now. The sweat was pouring off his face.

'You've written a lot of one star book reviews,' she reminded him.

He just stared at her. He was clutching his chest and breathing very heavily. He could no longer talk.

'I bet you don't even remember the reviews you wrote about my husband's books,' she said. She reminded him of what he had written. She didn't need to look them up. She knew the reviews by heart.

He stared at her. 'They were just reviews,' he managed to whisper. 'Call an ambulance! I need an ambulance.'

'My husband killed himself because of your reviews. And now you're going to die, here on the pavement.'

He mumbled something. Harriet bent closer. 'You're mad,' he spat.

'Possibly,' she agreed. 'But if I am then I'll still be mad tomorrow, whereas you will be a corpse.'

He stared at her disbelievingly. 'You're letting me to die because of some damned reviews I wrote?'

Harriet shook her head. 'I'm not allowing you to die,' she told him. 'I'm killing you. The capsule you took so eagerly contained the contents of six Viagra capsules. The glass ampoules contained amyl nitrate. The combination is deadly. As a result, you're now having a massive heart attack and you'll be dead within minutes. I will then walk away. When I've walked a mile or so I'll ring for a taxi from a public phone box. There's bound to be one in a pub somewhere. I'll travel to the station and I'll catch a train. No one will ever know that you were murdered and no one will ever know that I killed you. Even if the barman and the old men in the pub remember that we left together the police will just assume that you collapsed in the street, overcome by excitement, and that you died of a heart attack. I doubt if the pathologist will bother to do a full toxicology study on your body but if he does then he'll just assume that you took too much Viagra to boost your sexual performance. No one will look for me.' She paused. 'And even if they do look for me they'll never find me.'

He opened his mouth to say something but no words came out. There was saliva on his chin. He could no longer hold himself up. He collapsed completely onto the pavement. And in just another couple of minutes he was dead. It was a pity it was all over so quickly but Harriet was pleased that he'd known why he'd died.

She walked for a mile to another pub and used their payphone to ring for a taxi. While she waited for the taxi she went into the ladies lavatory and changed into a longer skirt. She also slipped into a pair of low heel shoes. She had the skirt and the shoes tucked into her laptop bag. She got rid of her spectacles. She removed most of her make-up.

The second killing had been just as easy as the first.

Chapter Eight

The next few weeks were hectic and exhausting. It was the travelling, not the killing, that Harriet found tiring. She remembered the Blues Brothers film and decided that she too was on a mission from God. It was work that had to be done and she was proud to do it. Every killing made her feel more comfortable and more at peace. At night she often talked to Mallory and told him how things were going.

In the Midlands she found a pseudonymous reviewer who worked as a traffic warden.

The woman had written scathing reviews of several of Mallory's books, boasting in one review that she had only read the first page of one book but had decided that since that single page hadn't 'tickled her fancy', as she put it, she was going to damn the other books too.

The day after identifying the reviewer, Harriet watched the woman preparing to give a ticket to the absent owner of a car parked outside a pharmacy. Before the traffic warden had started to photograph the car, in order to record the offence, a harassed young woman came rushing out of the shop. The woman, clearly a young mother, was carrying a small child who was crying and appeared to be in a lot of pain.

'I had to get some antibiotic medicine for my little boy,' said the woman, pleading. She was clearly close to tears. 'The car park is full and there was nowhere else to leave the car.' In desperation, she looked at her watch. 'I've only been here for three minutes.' She held up a paper bag which clearly contained medicine bottles and then unlocked her car and hurriedly fastened the little boy into a seat in the back.

The traffic warden, a small, slight, miserable looking woman, a professional giver of tickets and, Harriet knew, an amateur book reviewer, showed absolutely no emotion at all. She simply lifted up her camera, took the incriminating photographs she needed and ignored the woman's plea.

Harriet spent three days in the area finding out everything there was to find about the traffic warden. By the time she'd finished her researches she was surprised to discover that the traffic warden was an even nastier person than she had originally thought. The woman had absolutely no redeeming features and no friends. She lived alone in a small flat and even the other traffic wardens regarded her as unbearable. 'She is,' one told Harriet, 'the sort of person who would have been well suited to work in a concentration camp. She'd have quickly risen through the ranks to become Chief Torturer.'

Harriet discovered that every morning the traffic warden parked her car in a multi-storey car park owned by the local council. The car park was kept exclusively for employees of the council and the police station (which was next door to the main council building). Some days the traffic warden didn't start work until 10.00 a.m. and by the time she arrived, the lower floors of the car park were all full. So, on those days, she had to park her car on the top floor. There was a lift but it was slow and smelt of urine and excrement so, after parking her car, the woman usually walked down several flights of concrete stairs. On those mornings the car park was usually quite deserted since most employees were already sitting at their desks making paperclip chains and dreaming of their gloriously plump taxpayer funded pensions.

There were no security cameras in the car park; either because the council was too mean to install them or because council employees and policemen don't like being spied upon.

And so, on her fourth morning in the town, Harriet waited on the top floor of the car park and, when the little traffic warden started down the stairs she followed behind and gave her a tremendous push. She pushed her so hard that she very nearly toppled forward herself.

Concrete is a very unforgiving material, harder and more unforgiving than any traffic warden's head, and the warden, who had very little fat on her to cushion her fall, crashed and slid to the bottom of the staircase. It all happened so quickly that she didn't even have time to cry out.

Harriet walked down the stairs, knelt beside her victim and found, to her surprise and relief, that although the woman was badly injured she was still conscious. It would have been a terrible disappointment if she'd died too soon.

The woman had broken an arm and a leg and seemed to have dislocated her shoulder. She was in a good deal of pain. Harriet bent down beside her, introduced herself, told the woman who she was and talked to her for a while about the reviews the woman had written about Mallory's books.

The traffic warden didn't seem terribly upset about the damage she'd done and, to Harriet's dismay, seemed concerned only with her own situation rather than with the consequences of her literary actions or the effect her thoughtless words had had on Mallory. Struggling for breath and in considerable pain the woman accepted that she hadn't read any of Mallory's books and admitted, seemingly without regret, that she always gave books one star reviews.

Harriet helped the traffic warden to her feet (a manoeuvre which the woman seemed to find extremely painful and which resulted in quite a few cries of pain) and then rather surprised her by pushing her down the next flight of stairs. She hadn't seen that coming.

Harriet was rapidly running out of stairs and she was greatly relieved when she saw that this fall had finally killed the woman. She hadn't fancied the idea of having to drag her back up the stairs in order to throw her down them again.

From the way the traffic warden was positioned it was clear that she had broken her neck. She had also smashed her skull on the side of the stairs and you could see little bits of brain poking out. The brain tissue was much greyer than Harriet had expected it to be. Despite all these injuries there was hardly any blood at all; in death, as in life, the woman seemed a cold, bloodless sort of creature.

Harriet walked down the rest of the stairs, left the car park and walked to the railway station. She retrieved her bag from the left luggage locker and wasted £3.50 on a cup of coffee and a bun in the buffet. The bun was stale and she ate only half of it. The coffee was lukewarm and tasted more like weak gravy; she drank very little of it but resisted the temptation to complain to the counter assistant. She didn't want to do anything that might make her memorable.

The following day, Harriet looked at the local newspaper's website on the Internet and saw that the woman's death had been reported as a tragic accident. A police spokesman said they believed the traffic warden must have slipped on the concrete steps and they were investigating the possibility that uncollected litter, allowed to accumulate on the steps, might have contributed to the tragedy. He added that they would, in consequence, be investigating the possibility of charging council officials with contributory negligence. A council spokesman said they had taken advice from a senior Health and Safety officer who, in conjunction with a firm of consultants would, at the earliest possible date, have the steps covered in a 'non-slip plasticised material' that would 'prevent any future mishaps of a similar nature'. The spokesman also said that the council would install six litter bins on each floor of the car park and hire a firm of cleaners to do a twice daily litter collection in the car park. The traffic warden's death had, it seemed, been rather expensive for the local taxpayers.

 Harriet travelled south to Dorset where she was looking for a reviewer who hid behind the woefully unimaginative pseudonym 'Buyer', but whose real name was George.

Chapter Nine

George had been convicted of a series of frauds and had spent much of his life in prison. In his early life he had made his money by leeching off rich, older women. He had married three of them. His modus operandi was to persuade the unfortunate women that he was a much better investment consultant than any of the banks or brokers they were currently using and to persuade them to allow him to manage their money. He then moved all their wealth into his name, forging their signatures on the requisite documents.

Much of the money had all been spent on the usual mixture of fast cars, slow horses and fast women though he had also invested, generally unwisely, in property. He had at one point owned a chateau in the Loire valley and had spent much of the money he had acquired on an ill-fated and extravagant restoration project. The chateau had eventually been sold at a huge loss.

The big money had all gone and George's good looks and boyish charm had also disappeared. He had reinvented himself as an online Lothario. Pompous, patronising and unbearably superior in his online manner he considered himself to be an expert on a whole range of topics and worthier in every way to the authors whose books he so easily condemned.

George and his latest wife, Sharon, lived in a small semi-detached house on a rather dull looking estate.

Harriet found a small hotel in the town where George lived and, once again, found out as much as she needed to know by going door to door and posing as a marketing researcher.

George's wife, blonde and shapely, was much younger than her husband and not terribly bright. She had succumbed to what was left of George's charm but had, it seemed, soon regretted her trip to the registry office. She was in her mid-thirties, little more than half his age, and, after chatting to several of their neighbours, Harriet quickly discovered that she was having an affair with their landlord, an Asian gentleman who visited the house rather more frequently than might be considered strictly necessary. He usually managed to time his visits so that he called when George was out visiting the pub or the bookies.

One of the neighbours to whom Harriet spoke, a talkative and lonely woman in her sixties, told her that she suspected that Sharon telephoned him, or maybe sent him a text message, when the coast was clear. In the old days, a cheating spouse would put a vase in the bedroom window; things are so much easier these days.

Harriet discovered that George's wife was planning a weekend away with her lover. She had confided in one of the neighbours that the two of them were going away to Bournemouth for two nights. Her lover had, she said, booked a suite at one of the smartest hotels for what she had unashamedly described as their forthcoming 'dirty weekend'.

She'd told her unsuspecting husband that she had to travel north to visit her parents, both of whom were in poor health. George was far too sure of himself to suspect that he was being cuckolded.

Harriet was pleased that Sharon had a lover because she knew it meant she was unlikely to find widowhood particularly trying. From what she'd heard, she suspected that the Asian gentleman friend would leap at the chance to make the relationship more permanent. And she was pleased too that Sharon would be out of the way for a day or two. It would give her a chance to deal with George without what the military call 'collateral' damage.

The other piece of vital information Harriet acquired was that at this time of the year George was in the habit of walking on the nearby local common on Sunday mornings and collecting mushrooms. He would then take the mushrooms home, fry them with a couple of eggs and have them for brunch.

Mallory had always said that people who pick wild mushrooms must be lacking some essential part of their brain. He pointed out that the number of people who become seriously ill because they've picked a poisonous mushroom or two is really quite frightening and that merry mushroom pickers die with startling regularity. When Mallory was thinking of having a character die from mushroom poisoning, Harriet did some research and was astonished to find just how easy it must be to pick and eat a deadly mushroom. She could still remember a good deal of what she had learned.

Harriet put together all these tidbits of information and quickly came up with a scenario which seemed likely to work very well.

On the Sunday when Sharon and her lover were away entertaining each other in Bournemouth, Harriet visited the common where George did his foraging. But whereas he took a large plastic bag with him she took nothing in which to put her mushrooms. So when they met, apparently accidentally, she was holding her small collection of fungi in her gloved hands.

'Excuse me,' Harriet said, approaching the cuckolded walker. 'Are you collecting mushrooms?'

George said that he was, and opened his bag to show her the few mushrooms he'd collected. He had, she suspected, found most of his mushrooms growing in the grass or in fairly open woodland. Two of Harriet's had come from the grassland but the other two had been plucked from under a tree. And she hadn't chosen to wear gloves just because the weather was rather chilly.

'I picked these,' said Harriet, showing him the mushrooms in her hands. 'But I didn't bring a bag with me. May I pop them in with yours? I honestly don't know why I picked them because I can't use them but I can't bear to just throw them away – it would be such a waste.'

George was, predictably, delighted to accept the small donation. He smiled and turned on what was left of his charm. Harriet could not help noticing that, like most people who have been in prison, he talked without moving his lips.

When he had thanked her, George asked Harriet if she wanted to go home with him to share his brunch. He managed, without effort, to make it clear that it was more than brunch he was offering to share. Harriet apologised and said that she was afraid that she couldn't join him because she had arranged to visit a friend in hospital after she'd finished her walk. George was a great deceiver and it seemed appropriate that he should be about to die through a great deception.

The two then parted and wandered off in different directions.

Harriet threw her gloves into a waste bin, and pushed them underneath an old newspaper so that no innocent passer-by would see them and retrieve them. She took a carefully planned route and walked around the area until she ended up at the bottom of George's back garden. Through a small gap in the fencing she could see him in his kitchen, preparing his brunch of freshly picked mushrooms. He thought he was eating a pleasant mixture of field mushrooms, wood mushrooms and honey mushrooms. He probably was; but he was also eating two death cap mushrooms. It had taken Harriet three hours to find them. They look much like common, edible mushrooms. Eat just half of one of these mushrooms and you're going to die. There is no antidote. Even touching them can be deadly.

The death cap mushroom works in a strange way. Twelve hours or so after eating just part of one of these mushrooms a human being will develop diarrhoea, vomiting and muscle cramps. He will feel quite ill. But the symptoms will then disappear almost as quickly as they came and the victim will feel fine. He will assume that all is well. But it won't be. He may feel well, and may suspect that he has merely suffered a little unpleasant food poisoning, but he has less than a week to live. And the clock is ticking.

Four or five days after eating a death cap mushroom the victim will fall ill again. And this time there will be no recovery. The liver, heart and the kidneys shut down and stop working and the victim quickly dies. There is total organ shutdown. And short of putting in a completely new set of organs there is absolutely nothing that doctors can do. It is a particularly unpleasant death, and it is a lingering death, but George wasn't a particularly pleasant man so that was fine.

Harriet watched until George had finished eating and then she walked to the railway station. She really wanted to tell George that he was now going to die, and to explain why. But she couldn't risk doing that straight away because although doctors would not be able to help him there was clearly a chance that if she did so George would want to tell the police. And then the authorities would know that he'd been murdered and they would start looking for her. For now, at least, she had to allow George (and everyone else) to assume that the deadly mushrooms had been among the ones he'd picked himself. Even if he remembered the stranger who'd dropped her mushrooms into his bag there was no reason for anyone to suspect that the donation had been made with bad intentions.

So, Harriet left Dorset and headed towards the north of England where another unsuspecting reviewer was alive and well and living on borrowed time. She planned to come back in a few days to check on George. With any luck she would find a way to see him and to let him know that he'd been executed – and precisely why he'd had to die.

Chapter Ten

Harriet's target in the north of the country was a woman called Elizabeth who had downloaded several of Mallory's books (all of which were available free at the time). She had written scathing reviews of every one of them.

Harriet could remember, word for word, the review the woman had written of the first of Mallory's books.

'This sort of stuff is not my kind of thing. Laughably out-of-date and old-fashioned. No market for it these days. I downloaded it free so it didn't cost me a penny, thank heavens. I read half a page and deleted it.' The review was, of course, accompanied by a single star.

A little research showed that Elizabeth had written over 250 reviews. Every book she had reviewed had been given just one star.

Masquerading, as usual, as a market researcher (but this time dressed as a hippie, wearing clothes purchased from a local charity shop) it didn't take Harriet long to discover that Elizabeth was disliked and distrusted by just about everyone who knew her. She drank Guinness by the gallon and smoked 80 cigarettes a day. She paid for these unhealthy comestibles by shoplifting and was well known to the local police.

Elizabeth was a lesbian, lived in a caravan which was parked permanently but illegally on a scrap of waste land underneath a flyover and wrote her reviews on a computer which was one of three provided free of charge at a drop in centre run by a local charity. She paid nothing for the computer, nothing for the Internet connection and nothing for the books she downloaded.

The authors whose books she 'reviewed' paid a heavy price.

Harriet met Elizabeth in a local public house, a dingy wreck of a place where the walls still carried tattered posters advertising a Millennium New Year's eve party, and since the woman was already pretty drunk, Harriet had no difficulty in starting a conversation.

When the pub closed, Harriet accepted Elizabeth's invitation back to her caravan (which was, conveniently, parked no more than half a mile away from the pub). The doomed reviewer told Harriet that she had several packs of Guinness there. She may have imagined that she had made a conquest.

The caravan, which was the size of one of those contraptions which are popular with holidaymakers who like to tow their bedroom, living room, bathroom and kitchen behind their car, was old and battered outside and a disgusting mess inside. The bed, at one end of the caravan, was unmade and didn't look as if it had been made for a decade or two. The kitchen sink was full of empty beer cans and chip wrappings. The floor was so dirty that it made a scrunching sound underneath Harriet's feet.

Getting rid of Elizabeth was ridiculously easy; probably easier than getting rid of an annoying rodent. To be honest, Harriet would have never dreamt of killing a mouse, or even a rat, but she regarded killing Elizabeth as a valuable public service, one to which no sensible person could possibly object.

As soon as they entered the disgusting caravan, Elizabeth made a half-hearted pass at Harriet, but the reviewer was so drunk that it was easy for Harriet to deflect her. Harriet asked for a Guinness (a drink which she hated) and Elizabeth immediately opened two cans, handing Harriet one of the cans and putting the other on the crowded Formica top beside the sink. When she had done this, Elizabeth turned away to find her lighter. She then struggled for a minute or two to light a cigarette. As Elizabeth struggled with trembling fingers and a reluctant lighter, Harriet crushed a Rohypnol sleeping tablet between her fingers and dropped the powder into Elizabeth's can of Guinness.

Twenty minutes later Elizabeth was lying on her bed, almost unconscious. Rohypnol has been described as the 'rape drug' because it paralyses people – and makes them incapable of resistance. Those who take it become drowsy and confused.

Harriet asked Elizabeth if she remembered writing her reviews of Mallory's books. Naturally, she told the woman Mallory's pen name. Elizabeth couldn't reply but Harriet could see that she had no idea what she was talking about and so she reminded the paralysed woman of the words she'd written and told her the consequences. Elizabeth frowned and mumbled something incomprehensible. Harriet told her that her reviews had helped kill her husband and that now she too was going to die. There was panic in Elizabeth's eyes and she tried, unsuccessfully, to lift herself up off the bed. The pathetic woman's cigarette was still burning and Harriet gently moved her hand so that the cigarette was touching the filthy eiderdown on top of the bed. Within a minute, the eiderdown was smouldering. Harriet picked up an old newspaper and placed it on top of the eiderdown. That quickly burst into flames.

Harriet then said goodbye to Elizabeth, who now looked terrified.

Having no idea whether or not burnt beer cans retain fingerprints, Harriet took with her the opened can of Guinness, the only item in the caravan which she'd handled. She then emptied the Guinness onto the ground outside the caravan and walked away.

When she looked back a couple of minutes later she could see the flames inside; within a couple of minutes the whole caravan was ablaze. A few minutes later there was an explosion as a gas cylinder blew up. It was quite dramatic. Harriet stood for a moment and looked back. The whole area was quite deserted and it was dark. Harriet wiped the empty can on her skirt and tossed it into a puddle where it lay amidst a pile of other 21st century debris.

Chapter Eleven

Having dealt with Elizabeth, Harriet caught a late bus back into the town and stayed the night in her hotel.

The following morning, after breakfast, she headed for the station to catch a train heading back south. She bought a sandwich and a bottle of water at the station buffet (she had learned that although trains may advertise the presence of a buffet car it is always wise to assume that there won't be one) and waited for a moment to listen to the news being broadcast by the local radio station. Elizabeth's fiery death was the fifth or sixth item on the news, just before the sport. The newsreader said that firemen had been called to a blazing caravan but had been unable to save the sole occupant. A fire brigade spokeswoman was reported as having said that the blaze was probably caused by a cigarette and that it was believed that the deceased woman had been drinking heavily. Harriet's visit to the North of England had been both successful and mercifully brief and when she returned to Dorset, she was pleased to find that George was still alive. He was, however, still dying, of course, and the doctors had given up trying to save his life. There was clearly no point in wasting valuable health service resources on a man who was doomed. There had apparently been some talk for a day or so about a kidney transplant and one ambitious doctor had told a reporter from the local radio station that they were looking for a replacement liver to pop in. But then George had a heart attack and it was clear that he would need a whole body transplant if the doctors were going to keep him alive.

The death cap mushroom is a marvellous asset for anyone who needs to get rid of a human pest and the fact that the dying individual takes some time to reach the end can, in the appropriate circumstances, be something of a bonus.

Harriet was well pleased with the result of her mushroom picking expedition, though she was saddened to realise that she wouldn't be able to use this particular method again for at least a year. She knew it was important to make sure that no possible pattern emerged. Even

Britain's woeful police forces might sit up and take notice if one of the national tabloids ran a front page 'splash' warning of a national epidemic of death by mushroom poisoning.

George was in a bed in the local hospital's Intensive Care Unit. Harriet thought it rather a waste of a valuable bed, since everyone involved, right down to the cleaners, knew that George was on a one way trip to the morgue, but she realised that the doctors probably felt that since there was absolutely nothing they could do, they ought to make some sort of effort to disguise their ignorance and ineffectiveness.

Harriet had expected the widow-in-waiting to be sitting at the dying man's bedside but she was quietly pleased when she found that she and her Asian fancy man had not bothered to wait for George to take his last dying gasp before setting up house together. From what she'd learned she felt that Sharon, although a simple young woman, was a pleasant creature. Sharon had moved into her lover's large, detached home and the house she and George had shared was already being advertised as available for rent. The neighbours were talking of little else and there was even some talk that Sharon might have herself been responsible for picking the death cap mushrooms. Harriet was relieved when the widow-to-be managed to provide herself with an excellent alibi (the hotel staff remembered her and her lover very well) and to avoid, therefore, any unpleasantness with the authorities. Sharon was not, perhaps, the sort of woman ambitious mothers would want as a daughter-in-law but she didn't deserve to be locked up for murdering her husband when she'd done nothing of the sort.

The absence of the widow in waiting meant that Harriet could easily totter into the hospital and sit herself down at George's bedside. No one asked what she was doing there. One young nurse, plump and red cheeked, said 'hello' and Harriet had a little word with her and thanked her for everything they'd done. The nurse looked about sixteen. Harriet told the youngster that she'd like to express her thanks and asked if she and her colleagues would prefer a box of biscuits or a box of chocolates. The nurse blushed and said she thought that they'd prefer chocolates and so Harriet told her that before she left the hospital she'd pop into the shop and ask them to deliver some chocolates to the Intensive Care Unit. She promised that she wouldn't forget. Harriet had never liked people who promised to do things and then forgot about them.

The nurse explained that George couldn't move or speak but that the doctors thought that he could hear perfectly well and that if Harriet wanted to give him a final message he would be able to understand her. Harriet really couldn't have asked for more.

Harriet sat beside the dying man and held his hand (the one that didn't have the drip in it) and told him who she was. She reminded him that they'd met when he'd been picking mushrooms and she told him that it was she who had put the death cap mushrooms into his little bag. She said she felt it was a pity that they couldn't talk together but she told George that his pathetic little one star reviews had played a part in her husband's death and that it seemed apt that they were now the cause of his own demise. Harriet was sure that she could tell by the look in his eyes that he could hear her and that, although he was startled and puzzled, he understood what she was telling him.

Harriet felt sorry for the nurses who had to look after George as he lay dying. It could not have been easy; indeed it must have been a difficult job for them. It was, she thought, typical of George that even in the manner of his death he should cause such pain and distress to those around him.

On her way out of the hospital, Harriet called into the hospital shop and paid for a large box of Black Magic chocolates. Then just before she left, she noticed that they had some chocolates called Celebrations. She paid for a box of those too, and the nice assistant behind the counter said she'd send both boxes up to the ITU. Harriet didn't give her name. It didn't seem either necessary or a terribly good idea. Even if they remembered her visit, the staff would merely consider her to be a relative, a neighbour or, perhaps, a mistress.

Harriet rang the hospital later that evening and someone with a kind and sympathetic voice told her that George had passed away.

Chapter Twelve

There was still much to do, of course.

Harriet knew that she had hardly begun what she now thought of as her mission. She had learned that one star reviewers are very easy to kill. She knew that the hours, days, weeks and months ahead would be long and sometimes arduous. There would be a lot of travelling, a good deal of poor food and a good many lumpy beds. But the killing would be easy. And she had worked out that their savings and the money she would get for the sale of their house would enable her to continue with her mission for some years to come.

The following morning, Harriet was sitting in the hallway of the small hotel where she had been staying. She was waiting for a taxi to arrive to take her to the station. The hotel was simply furnished but neat and spotlessly clean and very good value. As she sat, waiting, Harriet overheard the owner and his wife talking about a review that someone had posted on an Internet site which encourages customers to publish their comments about hotels, restaurants, theme parks and places open to the public. It appeared that a guest who had attended a wedding held at the hotel had written a scathing review after being asked to leave the premises. He had been drunk, had sexually assaulted two waitresses and had thrown several pieces of garden furniture and a number of pot plants into the hotel swimming pool. He had done a considerable amount of damage to the reception area.

The bride and the bridegroom had both agreed that the guest, who was a black sheep relative from the bride's side, should be asked to leave the premises. But, entirely out of spite, the unwelcome guest had more than got his own back by subsequently publishing a vicious and, it was clear, entirely unjustifiable review on a site called Trip Advisor. Harriet had never heard of the site but she gathered that it was widely used and quite powerful. The owner's wife was crying. The owner, trying to comfort her, was struggling to hold back his tears.

Harriet talked to the couple who told her that they were by no means the only people in their situation. They said they knew of several hoteliers who were desperate to leave the business they were in because they were constantly terrified that a vindictive customer might give their establishment a bad review.

'We know someone who got two bad reviews and found out that they had been written by a competitor,' said the hotel owner. 'The accusations which were made were entirely false but what can you do?'

'A man we know used to run a restaurant but he had a heart attack because of worrying about reviews on the Internet,' his wife told Harriet. 'People mark you down for all sorts of things. He got a terrible review from a couple who had dinner at his restaurant and then found that their car, which had been left parked in the street, had been damaged by someone scratching a key across the paintwork. It wasn't his fault but when he refused to pay for the damage to the car the couple went on every site they could find and wrote rude things about him and his business. How can you cope with things like that? Just waiting for the next spiteful review is no sort of life.'

Harriet was appalled. She looked at the name of the guest who had written the awful review of the hotel. She remembered that Deborah, the first reviewer she had deleted, had been an enthusiastic user of the TripAdvisor site. And so, indeed, had several of the other reviewers she'd had to deal with. One had told her that he gave one star reviews to many hotels and restaurants he'd never visited simply because he didn't see why anyone in business should enjoy free publicity which might help them to make money.

'Do you have an address for this guest?' asked Harriet sweetly. 'He sounds like someone I know.'

The hotel owner nodded and checked his computer. 'Manchester,' he said. He turned the monitor so that Harriet could see the address. 'Oh no,' she said. 'It's not the person I was thinking of.' She memorised the address, smiled sweetly at him and said goodbye.

Twenty minutes later Harriet arrived at the railway station. She paid the taxi driver, giving him a small but not memorable tip, and strode purposefully directly to the ticket office. It had become natural for her to do everything she could to remain unnoticed.

'What is the time of the next train to Manchester?' she asked the man in the ticket office. She bought the cheapest second-class ticket available and walked to the buffet. She had three quarters of an hour to wait.

There were many busy days ahead.

After Manchester, she had to travel to London for there was still that young editor to be dealt with; the one who had rejected Mallory's books.

Harriet had the woman's home address and knew that she rode a bicycle to and from work, with part of her route taking her down a narrow alleyway. The alleyway passed near to a row of abandoned lock up garages which were awaiting demolition. The garages were in a very bad state and a nearby greengrocer had used a couple of them as a dumping ground for unsold produce. As a result, there were a number of rats in the neighbourhood. One of the garages still had useable doors which Harriet had decided she could lock with a padlock and a piece of chain.

Harriet's plan was simple. She would hide in the alleyway one evening and knock the young editor off her bicycle with a broomstick. She would then tie her to one of the beams, gag her (so that she couldn't cry out) and starve her to death. Harriet thought that if she gave the girl small amounts of water once or twice a day then she should be able to keep her alive for a month or so. Harriet wanted to keep the young editor alive for that long because she intended to read all Mallory's books to her, so that she could see what a huge mistake she made when she decided to let them go out of print.

She would, she thought, have to make sure that the rats didn't eat the girl to death before she'd finished reading her all of Mallory's books.

She sometimes worried about the amount of work she had to do, though she found her new work satisfying and she was looking forward to killing the young editor. It would be a real relief.

But first of all, she had to pop up to Manchester.

The End

'The world kills the very good and the very gentle and the very brave impartially. If you are none of these you can be sure it will kill you too but there will be no special hurry.'
Ernest Hemingway, 'A Farewell to Arms'
(46 one star reviews on amazon.com and 17 one star reviews on amazon.co.uk)

Printed in Great Britain
by Amazon